DRAGGING THE RIVER

Great you
made it
Down !
Best —
Trevor
April 11
2009
I'm So Happy
You're
Here

Dragging the River

A NOVEL BY

Trevor Clark

⎡N₁ ⎡O₂ ⎡N₁
CANADA

*Publisher's note: This book is a work of fiction. Names, characters, places and
incidents are either the product of the author's imagination or are used
fictitiously, and any resemblance to actual persons living or dead
is entirely coincidental.*

Library and Archives Canada Cataloguing in Publication

Clark, Trevor, 1955–
Dragging the river : a novel / Trevor Clark.

ISBN 978–0–9739558–5–9

I. Title.

PS8555.L373D73 2009   C813'.54   C2008–907425–4

Printed and bound in Canada on 100% ancient forest-free paper.

Now Or Never Publishing Company
11268 Dawson Place
Delta, British Columbia
Canada V4C 3S7

nonpublishing.com
Fighting Words.

To Maria for her sexy spirit,
and Jade, her ethereal coolness,
from Tiger Tiger to Graceland.

XX

"I am glad I have not had a scientific education," said Lamotte; "I have always thought, and shall continue to think, of women as a miracle of Nature."

—Robertson Davies, *The Rebel Angels*

We have seen the young man mutilated,
The torn girl trembling by the mill stream.
And meanwhile we have gone on living,
Living and partly living,
Picking together the pieces,
Gathering faggots at nightfall . . .

—T.S. Eliot, *Murder In The Cathedral*

"Before I had even got the needle out I could feel, you know, feel—Zzzoommm—a buzzing all over me, and I was feeling real, real good. The next thing I know I was back in my own room and it was morning. I had a gun, and I don't know where I got it. I just sat there wondering where the hell I got that gun."

—J. Altman and M. Ziporyn, M.D.,
Born To Raise Hell: The Untold Story of Richard Speck

Dragging the River

I

I avoid a panhandling drunk as I approach a dirty white brick hotel on the northwest corner of Dundas E. and Jarvis. The name of the Warwick glows in pink and green neon within flashing electric bulbs over the sidewalk, and again on the back of the building inside a framework of twinkling lights above the words, "Rooms, Showers, TV, Free Parking." The letter *e* of 'hotel' is a small window.

By the side door it advertises: "No Cover, No Minimum, Appearing Now, Strip Show, Girls, Nude Strip, Rooms $7.00 Per Person," and in a flourish of purple and white, "Strippers Revue."

In the smoky downstairs lounge men sit along a bar behind which naked women are painted on mirrors above the bottles. I pass the stage and continue down the far aisle to an empty table where I order a beer and scan the prostitutes assembled by the wall near the exit. An overhead light emphasizes the absolute placidity of a blonde staring at her drink. In a fluctuating society one thing seems consistent: the migratory return every night of the same nondescript women to their particular chairs.

How do they make their money? Once in a while I see men talking to them, but most seem rooted, except for the occasional piss, for thousands of stagnant hours. Just stirring and sipping. Can one pierce their barren expressions and move them to ecstasy, or are their pussies leather, their clits calloused?

"How's your hammer hanging, honey?" a voice bellows. "Yeah, *you*, baby!" I look over to see Brandy with his microphone poised in the spotlight. There is a drum roll, cymbals, organ music. When some men yell back, he fluffs his blonde wig and bats heavy lashes. "Hey, you mothers—how the hell are you?" The laughter and cheering doesn't impress him, however. He is a large, sequined portrait of scorn. His red lip curls dramatically. "Yeah, well, who the fuck *cares*?" A man gets up to say something with his glass in hand, gesturing to his crotch. "Jesus," Brandy snorts, "you couldn't get laid in a whorehouse." Snapping his fingers and tapping his foot, he launches into a rough and tumble "Hello, Dolly."

I drink my beer as I watch this middle-aged drag queen in his flowered dress and high heels, wondering how he feels to have reached what seems the pinnacle of his career before such an undistinguished audience. When he finishes his song he introduces the first dancer of the set. "Come on, you fuckers! The more you clap, the more Kitty'll take off for you!"

Always willing to support an underdog, I join the mild applause for this plain, thirty-something-year-old with teased hair. Is she actually bored stiff or merely defensive, perpetuating a cycle of unpopularity?

During the next break I decide to talk to that blonde near the back. Before I can sit down she asks me if I want to go out? "I don't know yet," I answer, pulling up a chair. "How much?"

"Fifty dollars."

"I only have twenty-five."

"Sorry."

I've never approached a whore before, and am more or less just making conversation with the natives. Perhaps a little levity is required. "I thought I might get a discount before the rush."

She smiles, barely. "It doesn't work that way."

The next day I go to my job at a publisher's warehouse in Don Mills on the northeast side of the city. There are modern factories, depots, offices, low-rise buildings with landscaped lawns. I'm lost in canyons of books as I push a wooden cart on the side of which my name is printed in magic marker on bright red tape. I have a pencil and some papers listing in computerized type the merchandise I'm required to select from the shelves and place in my wagon. I check them off as I move from aisle to aisle.

When my task is complete I transfer the books from my cart to a long table with my signed order, then take another form out of the box and push my wagon to the first row on either side of the warehouse, depending on the percentage of hard covers or paperbacks specified on the list, and begin another journey.

A number of my coworkers are women of East Indian-Guyanese background who talk secretly among themselves. The supervisor of the hard cover section is a fastidious introvert in his early forties named Peter: a mathematics graduate and astronomy enthusiast surviving in quiet desperation between the books and stars. I listen to his gossip and the hushed resentments he has towards his hefty, overbearing cousin Walter, the warehouse manager.

There are other losers in their twenties like me in the paper-back department, a black guy named Sam works the scales, and grizzled old Hank, a boozer from the Maritimes, runs shipping and receiving.

Since dropping out of university I haven't managed to get my foot in the door of anything in the way of a career, and have just been drifting. It's August, 1980. Originally I was thinking of this as an indirect route into the editorial department, but discovered that the main offices are in the UK, and opportunities here are limited.

In the late afternoon heat I join the rush hour crowd on the bus, and head home to the Hotel Isabella: a dark, neo-Victorian structure on Sherbourne just south of Bloor, with turrets and a relatively hip if seedy reputation due in part to the punk bar in the basement and the Cameo blues room upstairs. Across the street, east to Parliament, is a concentration of slummy high-rises known as St. Jamestown.

Picking up a newspaper and submarine sandwich, I go upstairs. People have written bad poetry on the walls, and scrawled such things as "Carol & Dean" in ball-point pen where I've taped up handbills for local bands and other items collected during my travels, such as "Max's Kansas City, NYC," and "Redlight Theatre Presents *Strange Games*." There's an early photo of John Lennon in Hamburg on the back of the pink closet door. My underwear and socks are visible in the top drawer of the bureau, since the board fell off and now stands propped against the radiator. There's no light switch in the bathroom; one has to unscrew the bulb by hand.

I read the paper on my bed and while away some time with an old atlas. Turning to China, I examine that vast pink terrain inscribed with cities, towns and rivers. Then I go to the next page, inspecting a purple Thailand, an orange Laos, a green North and South Vietnam, a yellow Cambodia, and daydream about such exotic locales before realizing that they're probably still gutted by war.

Cut across and scan Australia, Borneo and New Guinea. The distance between points is gauged in broken red lines which intersect with white longitude and latitude stripes. Why, there's Tahiti. The southern chunk of planet is sprinkled with thousands of islands, any one of which may have harboured shipwreck survivors, escaped convicts, buried treasure, cannibals, missionaries and leper colonies.

I search for a place to which I could escape among the infinite array of paradises, charted like so many stars in the universe. Pondering their names, nationalities and geographical qualifications, I check the symbols on the scale beneath to discover that many of these locations are occupied by "Administrative Centres," presumably a euphemism for military installations. I can picture rowing a boat to shore moments before my world disappears in a flash of nuclear light.

Starbuck Island is a British-American possession south of the equator about 6 degrees latitude, 156 degrees longitude west of Greenwich, if I'm not mistaken. I look up a map of the world to see if it merits classification. Spotting it among the constellation of Line Islands, I wonder if my minute particle of jungle remains untouched with white sands, balmy breezes, angelfish about the coral. Maybe it's a radar station, an ugly heap of rocks marred by graffiti and sea gull shit.

My tattoos may also suggest the exoticism of the south seas and beyond: a palm tree, blue and purple Saturn, a bottle of whiskey, pink and black dice, crescent moon, multicoloured serpent, a woman's head in profile with golden, cascading hair.

"I Want To Hold Your Hand" comes on the radio, and I turn up the volume. The Beatles were once my greatest heroes and their songs embody my culture, my fucking roots. Lennon said he always needed a drug to survive, which suggests that an artist's awareness is both his gift and affliction, in that it might grant him access to difficult ports but also renders him vulnerable to the necessary means of escape.

Lying on my back, I look at the web that crosses my room a foot beneath the ceiling, linking sprinkler pipes along opposite walls. It's a curiosity I wouldn't any more destroy than a delicate artifact. There is no spider. The longevity of this singular thread is remarkable considering that two housekeepers who visit me on Fridays also leave it intact. They scrub my bathroom, vacuum, take out the garbage, change sheets and towels, yet the line continues to run silvery by the glow of the light bulb.

2

I go back to the Warwick's lounge with Sean Cochrane. Despite the disquieting nature of his intense blue eyes and the greasiness of a snake coiling around a knife below his rolled-up sleeve, he is soft-spoken and has the self-possession to sublimate his occasional moodiness. His brother, on the other hand, is serving time in Kingston Penitentiary for beating someone to death.

We're sitting a few tables back from centre stage, watching the first of a stripper's three dances. Nothing has come off yet. The plan is to pick up a couple of prostitutes, a route he's apparently taken before.

"I was walking through Kensington Market today," he says, turning to me, "and I saw two cats fucking in an alley. I always thought they were more private about that kind of thing."

"I once saw two cats fucking in the middle of a party."

"Well, these two were on their sides, and it looked strange." He raises a cigarette between two nicotined fingers and tosses his thin blond hair. Exhaling, he gives me a faint smile. "Twenty minutes later, I walked by again and saw the girl cat still lying there. I went over to look, and all these flies were buzzing around her."

"What, she was dead?"

"Yeah, the whole time."

I'd met him years earlier through a mutual friend, but I guess we've become better acquainted in recent times through speed. He's taken one or two junk cures and since drifted back to his first love, crystal meth, which I far prefer to heroin myself. I don't have any sympathy for junkies who deliberately had to work their way through countless boring and often nauseating highs to develop a habit. As far as I'm concerned, scag is more an image to be cultivated than a pleasure in itself. On one hand it's been suggested that junk is only really enjoyable after you become addicted, then every hit is a ray of sunshine. On the other, that the good times end once you've acquired that monkey, at which point it simply becomes painkiller. I only indulge when there's nothing better to do.

"A friend of mine broke up with his girlfriend yesterday," he says. "This lesbian punk with purple hair who was into S&M. She worked in a brickyard in the Don Valley."

I take a sip of beer, waiting for the rest of it.

"She said he was her first man. She just wanted to see what a guy would be like. She used to get him to smack her around with a billy club while she was tied to the bed, and was already bruised all over when he met her. Lester would have to beat the piss out of her just to get her in the mood, which began to make him nervous. You know, he was afraid he was accidentally going to kill her and get arrested as some freak."

Cochrane laughs as he reaches for his bottle. "How could he explain a naked woman tied to his bed that he beat to death with a fucking club?"

During the next break a bearded black guy about thirty-eight overhears us discussing the whores from the next table. He leans over and says, "You want a girl, eh? M'have a nice white chick. Me used to pay but now it's free. Even if she workin', she stop an' come with me." His teeth flash in a broad grin. "Me can grind an' grind for an hour if me want." He takes a small tube from his pocket and hands it to me. "The white mon needs help, so I len' you dis."

"What is it, saltpeter?"

"Yeah, mon, desensitizin' cream. It make me las' over two hours." He nods at a woman sitting a few tables away. "See that chick over there? Me screw an' screw her til she pass out. It nine inches long."

Cochrane is amused, and suggests that he prove it.

"Sure mon, in the washroom later. She tell me to stop, she say to me, 'I can't take it, I'll give you your money back. You must be West Indian.' Dem charge so much, me must get m'money's worth. But me say, 'Forget it.' After twenty-five, dem wrung out, dem can't las'."

The guy pauses and looks around. He's wearing a colourful shirt and a couple of medallions. "One time me come upon a black chick in dis place and she say, 'You a cop?' 'No,' I tell her. 'How much?' So she say, 'Fifty dollars.' Me warn her, 'Make it twenty, dahlin', or you get busted.' She say, 'Okay.'"

He puts the tube back in his pocket. "I'll ask dat hooker how much she charge tonight."

Before we can answer, he gets up and goes over to the brunette whom he fucked unconscious. As soon as he sits down, however, she tells him something and he stands up again. When he comes back, he looks nonplused. "Before I can open m'mouth, she say she not interested."

A little later we drink up and say good-bye. I walk down the dimly lit right aisle towards the back, where the same slim blonde I talked to couple of nights earlier is sitting in the corner. She looks at me without expression and asks, "Do you want to go out?"

I take the chair opposite her. "Yeah. A friend and myself thought we'd get a room together with you and your girlfriend over there, if that's okay with you."

She looks across the tables to Cochrane and the other blonde. "Um, yeah, I guess so, if it's okay with her."

They come over, and we discuss the plan. It seems the prostitutes working this bar use a different hotel a few blocks north, so they ask us to decide on a name under which to register. This way they can call for the room number after we check in, then catch a cab to meet us.

We take his white '67 Mustang up Jarvis. It's usually a fairly congested street with alternating lanes at peak hours, but is now comparatively quiet. There are very few stores, just buildings and the odd hotel or rooming house. We pass some dolled-up action at Gerrard where hookers are strutting and posing at each corner of the intersection. Outside Harvey's hamburger joint three of them hustle southbound traffic.

Sean turns east onto Carlton and drives to Larry's Hideaway, a run-down Cabbagetown dive not far from the fabled greenhouse and petty crime of Allan's Gardens. There are some bushes, trash and overgrown weeds by the fire escape. Old handbills and posters are plastered across the wall and nearby light standards for punk and new wave bands like The Fleshtones and Teenage Head, who play in the hotel bar.

Sean and I pay for a double at the front desk, then go down the first floor hallway, passing people wandering in and out of parties. We have a small room with smudged white walls, two beds, and a lavatory with an open door connecting us to the vacant next suite. A few minutes later, the women call to let us know that they're on their way.

When they arrive, mine tries to establish order by suggesting that we get the money out of the way. Standing there in the hard light in her minidress and heels, I see she's at least ten years older than I, a weather-beaten thirty-five or so with bleached hair and powdered pockmarks. Not bad looking, but under different circumstances I wouldn't have glanced at her twice, let alone paid her. Cochrane's whore is a little nicer. Bigger boned, but less worn. Maybe I didn't fully appreciate the equalizing power of money, that I could have aspired to someone prettier and not merely sympathetic. Ironically, after we all undress, I realize that any bond I felt was misplaced when she walks over to the sink and announces, edgy and authoritative, that it's wash-up time. Then with a marked lack of interest she soaps and dries off my flaccid prick. Cochrane seems no more aroused by the indifference of his girl.

Afterwards, on the beds, they suck us erect and roll onto their backs, drawing us on top. Mine discourages any reciprocal caressing, but I don't want to lose my mood by arguing about it, so I do what's required. The other one dampens my friend's ardour by suggesting that he just be quiet and enjoy himself. Perhaps it's against union rules to let tricks become overly familiar, since it may not be sanitary or profitable to be spoken to, kissed or aroused oneself. They keep their heads turned, avoiding superfluous contact. When we more or less ejaculate at the same time, the other prostitute declares it a photo finish, and informs us that one guy will usually come first and then watch the other one.

Pulling on my pants, I comment that I've never spent a faster fifty bucks. My hooker retorts that you get what you pay for, but I probably could have got myself off for free with more spirit.

3

A few nights later I'm looking at my pinpoint pupils in the subway window with my legs crossed and hands folded, hoping I won't be sick until the next station. Leaning harder against the side of the car to try and quell my nausea, I scratch my ribs and wipe the perspiration from my face. This will be the seventh time I've vomited since doing the hit, and my third unscheduled stop. For the first hour I thought I was going to be fine, but with my initial trip to the guy's washroom I recognized the debilitating pattern: once I puke on heroin, I keep puking.

By the time the northbound subway hits Wellesley station, I'm holding the pole, trying not to heave, and go out and prop myself against the green tiled wall. People walk past me towards the escalator as the train pulls away. There is a high-pitched metallic screech while it picks up speed, heading into the tunnel.

Slowly going to the south end of the platform, I step over a small gate by the sign prohibiting my entry, then make my way down the stairs to retch in the shadows. There is a Styrofoam coffee cup and some cigarette butts at my feet. As another wave rolls over me and I eject a few more nasty drops, a mouse scurries along the grimy concrete, pauses, and then darts under the rail.

According to family legend, one of my ancestors was a knight who participated in the killing of Saint Thomas à Becket in the year 1170.

My father's grandmother on his old man's side was a Barham, and her husband a Courtney like myself. The Barham line is on the verge of extinction with my late grandfather's cousins—an elderly woman in England, and her brother in Vancouver. He wrote a letter to my grandmother concerning this historical event, which she passed along to me, and from which I quote the following:

" . . . The Barhams have one major claim to distinction. We are descended from Reginald Fitz Urse (Son of the Bear) who was one of the knights responsible for murdering Saint Thomas à Becket. The family coat of arms is three black bears with gold muzzles, and the motto is *Le bon temps viendra*, which I suppose could be translated into 'There's a good time coming.'

"Actually, we never worried much about family in contradistinction to my mother who was Devonshire. My grandfather was in the raw silk trade with China and had a wonderful collection of Chinese porcelains, which my grandmother, who didn't care a hoot about such things, managed to break up as her eyesight failed in old age. He unfortunately became an alcoholic and died quite young. She hated him, wanted to marry the village blacksmith.

"They had six children—my father, Lydia (who was headmistress of a girls' school where they wore Kate Greenaway frocks and lace mittens), Rose, Alec's mother Emily (who married a milkman), and Bert, the youngest. He disliked his father, so Grandma loved him and left him the family silver service that should have come to my father and me. He always pointed it out and said it was mine, but his wife died and he sold everything, which annoyed Florence very much! Then there was Willie who died of scarlet fever.

"The previous generation were grocers in the city of London. Two of my great grandfathers were freemen of the city, members of the Court of Common Council. I have the Freedom presented to one of them. Grandma's mother, Granny Mugford, was a tough old biddy who, when Father was a boy, used to drive in her carriage out to hear General Booth who was starting the Salvation Army. She never contributed, just sat and chuckled as the sinners went up to the penitents' bench.

"Prior to that, at the time they were enclosing the commons, there was an eggler—a guy who bought eggs cheap from farmers' wives and sold them yard goods at extortionate prices, who managed to enclose a sizable chunk of common land and ended up as landed gentry.

"What a bunch! But our pride is Reginald Fitz Urse. Every time I am near Canterbury I go into the Cathedral, and in the Martyrdom just behind the high altar is a contemporary wall painting showing Reggie at his dirty work. I gaze in admiration . . ."

Given my family history while I'm puking on these subway tracks, I am drawn to the possibility that perhaps electricity off the third rail short-circuits my mind and first sparks the notion of assassinating the President of the United States of America. Oh, my magnetic field is shot. When I straighten up again, my eyes are watering. I wipe the sweat from my forehead and slowly climb the steps, hoping I might make it back to my hotel room without any more trouble.

To unravel the origins of my own destiny: I believe from a corroborating photo that my first memory took place at the age of three while walking with my parents in a winter field. I was snug in my cute little snowsuit and darling hat and warm mittens. *The camera pans across the ground with wide-angle lens. I paint the picture with broad strokes, blurring the canvas about the edges with linseed oil:*

I fell down and called out to my mother who was walking ahead. She turned around and told me to hurry in her tolerant but decidedly firm voice. No, I wanted her to come back and pick me up—I was a wee fellow. My father faded into oblivion. I realized the absurdity of my request when my mother, her tone slightly impatient, insisted that I come along right now, so I huffed and puffed and mustered my strength in my fussed little leggings and stood up, plodding my way through the snow. I was not embittered, as I was aware that I was behaving like a baby.

I've heard it said that none of our childhood memories are accurate because they've been filtered through years of dreams and self-deception, so there's no choice but to take each of my anecdotes with a large grain of salt.

I've been cracking up for a while and having the most distressing revelations. Beliefs I've held sacred are atrophying. For example, I just realized that nobody dies of old age. I always thought the majority of people passed away pleasantly in their beds due to their advanced years, and that the miserably unfortunate who kicked off beforehand from disease, coronaries and murder were victims of unforeseen circumstances hindering the Great Plan. But, in fact, those individuals who manage to die peacefully while asleep at ninety-eight are succumbing to heart attacks as well.

Nature doesn't take care of anyone's death in a dignified fashion, which is my final testament to God's nonexistence. Nothing is safe. A human corpse gives vent to sickening gases; its eyes become as glassy as that of any other carcass in the animal kingdom. You can toss it around, drag it behind your chariot, refuse to bury it and watch it picked apart by wild dogs, vultures and maggots.

In the heat of the sun one's lovely grandmother might lie in a meadow and raise the most frightening stench, causing one to cry at the brutality of this life, which isn't worth a plugged nickel when all the dignity a good soul can muster is constantly undermined by forces intent on reducing us to a state of putrefaction.

Another fact with which I have come to terms is the complexity of a mother's love. I never believed until recently that she was capable of preferences for certain offspring, but of course she is. If women can abandon babies at birth, we can assume they're not so blinded by maternal instinct as to ignore the qualities of the little beasts they've unwittingly nurtured through morning sickness and expelled with great pain onto the filthy carpet.

4

Early Saturday afternoon as I return to the hotel with some fish and chips, I get word from the desk that Izzy Silver called. When I phone him back he asks if I'd like to visit a mutual friend, Don Waters, who's serving a few months for the joint possession of four pounds of hash oil. About an hour later I go out to his hatchback, which is half up on the sidewalk but still impeding traffic, and meet a buxom blonde with smoky sunglasses in the passenger seat. "Lane, this is Tia Maria," he says. "She's a hooker."

I say hello and climb into the back, adding, "That's not a very gallant introduction."

"It's all right," he assures me, rocking behind the wheel. "Hey, tell him how much you make."

"Guys pay me two hundred dollars an hour," she says, yawning. "Tricks like ambassadors and judges."

She is attractive but lacks what I imagine would be considered upper income beauty. Hers is more a brassy allure. Although details on the grapevine were sketchy, I assume that she is one of the two bisexual party girls he was rumoured to have somehow hooked up with.

He puts on gaudy cartoonish shades with purple frames, and glances into the rear-view mirror as we pull out into traffic. "She's going to kiss Don and pass a couple of reds from her mouth to his."

When I mention that we'll probably have to talk through a window, he says that it's minimum security.

Izzy is something of a character. Childlike, excitable, stubborn, often cranky or manic, that peculiar brand of goof who manages to redefine behaviour that's acceptable. He treads a fine line between comic relief and that which might almost be called cool, due to the fact that he sold good drugs from a very young age. Anti-Semitic greaseballs who beat on nebbishes viewed him with a sort of perplexed respect, and invited him to their parties. His parents' house had been raided by police with dope-sniffing dogs, and he once made the newspapers after leading a chase on his motor scooter, crashing, rolling under a cruiser, and refusing to be treated in hospital.

I remember that he'd once looked in the window of a Halloween party and realized he needed a costume, so he punched two holes in the bag for his wine and went in with it over his head. He was also involved in the overdose of another friend, on which I'll elaborate later.

Although he has toned down sufficiently over the past few years to achieve a relative dignity, it doesn't explain the attraction of these two bad women who appear to be able to afford their own drugs. Since they were strangers unacquainted with his history or local reputation, I would have imagined that he would have come across at best as quirky.

At the detention centre we're told that Waters has already had his quota of visits for the week and isn't available, despite Izzy's claim to be a rabbi. He probably would have gagged on the Seconals anyway, since he wasn't expecting a strange woman to French kiss him, let alone a couple of barbiturates down his throat.

On our drive back to the Isabella, I pick up some beer and invite them up to my third floor room for a drink. There is a faint hint of exterminator spray in the staircase.

Izzy, sitting on the bed, is going through one of my photograph albums when I hand them their bottles. He complains that I don't have any pictures of him, so I go to my closet and bring out my camera. He wants to know how much film I have, then offers to buy it from me if I shoot the entire roll on them. I say fine, as long as I'm the one who gets it developed so that I can make copies.

Posing the two of them for a number of shots that utilize light from the window, I pause between frames to suggest that Tia take off her top for an avant-garde perspective. I'm just making conversation, but without batting an eye she starts undoing the buttons of her denim shirt. I hadn't noticed that she wasn't wearing a bra. Izzy suddenly laughs and runs a hand through his unruly curls. "Look at those big tits. I don't know what she sees in me."

"You're cute," Tia says, bored. Her full breasts sag slightly as she turns to drape the Levi's top over a chair. When she takes a swig of beer and looks at the lens, her face has an implacable hardness but her nipples are erect.

Izzy, wearing a blue V-necked sweater over a peach dress shirt, faces me and leans on his hand, his thick lips set determinedly, a few pimples or something on his forehead. I continue for another ten pictures before stopping to propose that we take the last five outside in case the others are underexposed.

After she gets dressed again we leave the old building and walk south along Sherbourne, going around the bar patio to Isabella Street. Without any prompting, Tia reopens her blouse in full view of whatever pedestrians or cars might be going by. I glimpse a few dumbstruck expressions and sense people at their windows as I set up. In the dazzling sunlight her boobs are not only goose-pimpled by the breeze, but are the centre of the universe. As I shoot the remaining film, she puts a hand on her hip and says, "I don't want these to go into a magazine or anything."

"Don't worry, it's just a private session."

Later that day after I've dropped the roll off for developing, I get a call from Izzy who tells me that she suggested I meet them upstairs at the Beverley Tavern on Queen Street W. around nine-thirty.

That evening grizzled locals inhabit the main floor drinking draft and watching TV while new wave bands pound it out overhead. I go up there to find the two of them with a couple of other people about a third of the way back from the stage. Izzy takes me aside and tells me that Tia's roommate Sandra will be arriving soon, but I mustn't come on to her because she's his. I didn't talk to him long enough to find out to what degree he's technically involved with either of them.

At some point I smoke some dope in the washroom with a couple of strangers, then return to our table where I try to talk to Tia over the music. So far she hasn't said anything to acknowledge that she'd indirectly invited me. It's agreed, however, that the three of us will go to the El Mocambo with some other people the next night to catch a punk act.

A couple friends of mine wander in and sit at our table shortly before the girlfriend shows up. She is slim and long-haired, and unexpectedly reserved. Tia Maria flicks her cigarette as she leans over. "Sandra and I are lovers, but I'm bisexual. She's totally gay and just turns tricks for the money. We were going to have a marriage ceremony, but I broke it off because she gets jealous of the guys I bring home, and always tries to throw them out. We get into a lot of fights, but she's not that tough, really." She turns her head away to cough. "I'm a witch, by the way. I worship Satan."

Two or three beers later, I decide to try and talk to Tia alone, and follow her when she heads off to powder her nose. I pass her as she chats with someone at a table, and continue to the back of the room, up the steps, and into to the ladies' washroom ahead of her. The light is quite bright. Luckily, there's no one in there.

I'm combing my hair when she comes in.

"What are *you* doing in here?"

"Just waiting for a bus."

She walks into a cubicle, and without closing the door, pulls down her jeans and sits on the toilet. I go over and crouch before her while she urinates. She ignores me as I unbutton her blouse and take her large breasts in my hands, caressing them, gently tweaking her nipples. Meeting no resistance, I lean in and give each of them a suck. Somebody suddenly enters the washroom, and I rotate on my haunches, meeting the startled eyes of a girl who turns abruptly and leaves. When Tia finishing peeing and wipes herself, I say, "Why don't we go back to my hotel?"

"No, come up to the townhouse."

"The Isabella's closer. You live in Willowdale."

A mood for which I have no explanation transpires. "You live in a dump," she sneers.

Despite the validity of this I find myself offended. "You think you're pretty tough, don't you?"

She takes a swipe at my face. "Fuck off."

"Yes, you're very frightening."

Tia Maria, still on the toilet, swings both fists at me, and I manage to grab her wrists and pin them back over her head while she yells and thrashes. She must be pretty loud, because suddenly Izzy appears behind me and tries to push his way into the cubicle. "What's going *on*? Everyone out there can *hear* you."

I manage to shove him out and still keep her down. "Not much. I'm just telling your girlfriend what a brat she is."

Two waiters rush in, so I pick up my bottle and leave. I can hear her shouting for a bouncer as I walk through the bar. Putting my beer on the table, I say good-bye to the others, then head out the door and down the stairs.

The next morning Izzy calls as soon as I've put my phone back on the hook. "What were you doing last night?" he asks. "I couldn't *believe* it."

Sitting on the bed in my underwear, I feel lousy enough without hearing that I've breached even his code of conduct. "Yeah, I know—"

"You're just lucky she didn't catch up to you with that broken bottle."

"What?"

"After you tried to rape her and everything, she wanted to know why there weren't any bouncers there to protect her. She smashed an empty bottle on the edge of the table and went down the stairs after you. Sandra caught up to her and talked her out of it."

"Well, I'm sure I don't know what the fuck you're talking about. I never tried to rape her."

Izzy sighs, and then blurts, "She *told* everyone what happened, and how you tried to make her blow you. Anyway, look, she'll forget the whole thing if you just return the photographs and the negatives. You were just drunk, that's all."

I consider how to proceed. "Listen, I admit being in the ladies' room was stupid, but she's lying about the rest of it. We were having a little fun until we got into an argument. I wasn't trying to rape her."

"It doesn't matter. You were drunk."

"I wasn't drunk. Listen, think about it. My pants weren't down or even unzipped when you came in, were they? Obviously I wasn't trying to force anything on her. And her shirt was only undone, it wasn't ripped. We were talking about whose place to go back to, and for some reason ended up in an argument which got out of hand."

Izzy doesn't answer at first. Then he says, "Well, she's really, *really* convincing. She told everybody. I don't know who's telling the truth, but she just wants the pictures back, all right?"

"Yeah, yeah." I scratch my head. "I'm still taking a few copies, though. If that's a problem, you'll have to stall her while I get them replaced."

This seems to satisfy him until it comes up that I still plan to go to the El Mocambo that night. "But she'll *be* with someone," he protests. "Even if you're telling the truth, he'll have to stick up for her and pick a fight. It's not fair to him, and you'll probably get beaten up."

I respect his logic and uncharacteristic sensitivity, but say, "Look, I'm not going to start a hassle, but if I see her I may have to call her a liar as a matter of principle. I can't have her going around telling people I'm this would-be rapist."

His moan is despairing. I'm sorry for having to put him in this position.

Around ten-thirty I'm drinking with a few people in the bar of the neon palms while the singer writhes about in front of the rest of The Diodes. I don't see Izzy, but by eleven I notice that he and Tia Maria, Sandra and another guy have come in, and are sitting at a table by the back wall under a couple of posters.

Between sets I decide to pay them a visit. When I get over there, however, I find that the witch has gone to the washroom, so I take her chair.

"I figured you'd be around sooner or later," Izzy says unhappily.

"I'm not here to cause trouble, I just want to set the record straight." I turn to the clean-cut, brawny character beside me. "I guess you're here with Tia Maria."

"Yeah."

"Well, I'm sure she told you about last night, and I'd just like you to know that most of it's untrue. I just have to explain that to her, then I'll go."

"It doesn't matter to me," he says.

When she returns, she demands that they leave.

"Don't go on my account," I say. "I'm only here to call you a liar."

She sweeps around and smacks me across the face. I jump up and slap her back.

"Get out of my chair!"

"But you're on your way," I answer, sitting back down.

"It's okay," her boyfriend says, restraining her. "Let's go."

"I'm not going *anywhere*! Get out of my chair right *now*!"

"Sure, as long as you understand what I told you."

Tia Maria takes another swing and pops me again, so I get up and clip her with my open hand. The musicians hit their splintered notes as I walk back to my table.

5

My earliest memory of my prick as a separate entity occurred when my mother pointed to it during bath-time and held out the soap, telling me to wash myself down there. I don't remember her ever undertaking it herself, just the refusal.

According to my father, our home was a farmhouse earlier in the century. In fact, there was still an orchard across the street when I was a baby, before contractors bulldozed to build the rest of the neighbourhood. No photographs exist to substantiate this mythological forest of apples.

A sense of worldly injustice was established early in my life. Imagine the suburbs following a rainfall one afternoon in, say, June 1959. The sky is overcast but clearing, the grass lush and green. As I peddled my tricycle around the front porch, an occasional car splashed through puddles on the road.

I saw my friend Bobby on his lawn across the street, and wheeled myself to the steps and called out to him. We chatted while I rocked dangerously near the edge. With a flurry of arms I suddenly went crashing down the stairs, and my face collided with the stone walkway, cutting my lip and chipping my tooth. Making me cry.

A week or so later I learned how to carry my tricycle off the porch so that I could ride elsewhere without requiring any help. I was sitting in the same position, watching my father garden beneath, when I attempted to make small talk by casually mentioning that I knew how to get my three-wheeler down. He was busy, and said gruffly like a son of a bitch, "Well, don't show me. Stay up there."

So I was rocking back and forth, merrily abiding by his decision, and for the second time ventured too close to the edge and lost my balance. I went barrelling down the steps, and was about to crack my skull when the old man caught me in mid-flight. Vast realities occurred within the next instant as my tricycle crashed. I have to laugh, considering my grasp of irony as he swung me to the path and set me on my feet, because I spontaneously cowered and shielded my head from the hard smack which shot stars before my eyes. I believe his violence overlapped any guilty gesture on my part.

"I *told* you not to take it off the porch!"

With a strangely cynical attitude for one so young, I didn't even bother trying to explain that I wasn't disobeying him, that he in fact saved me from pounding my face against the stones. To think that I had the presence of mind to shelter my cranium from the inhumanity which ruled the earth. Talk about a jaded sensibility.

But don't let a con artist arouse your sympathy. One day I was playing with Bobby and freckle-faced Doug beneath a bright sun. Our existence preceded civilization, circa 1960, and our minds were undeveloped. As a sparrow flapped helplessly about on the lawn, we gathered to watch its agonized dance, curious and solemn.

Doug wanted to know what was wrong with it.

"Maybe it's got a broken wing," I suggested. "Step on it."

Four or five years old, we pondered the matter.

"No, Lane—*you* step on it," Bobby answered.

Without any further ado I dispatched the bird with my foot. We continued to watch the sparrow's corpse, then walked away devoid of remorse. It appears in retrospect a brutal act. Was there a moral judgment in my rotten skull? Had I only wished to relieve the bird of its misery? What fascinates me was my total amorality. I recall stamping the sparrow without sadism, pity, or a flicker of thought.

My parents and I were to fly to New York City to visit their friends, then on to Maine to stay in a hotel on the ocean with my mother's relatives. The twins next door mocked my assertion that we were to take both an airplane and a helicopter, as they said 'copters were too small. While this was likely an early example of misinformation from my father, I still try to hold onto the possibility that there was something substantial in the plan, but we did, in fact, end up taking a second plane instead.

En route, in a minor exchange with my mother over Lake Ontario, I told her that I'd like to jump down into the blue water, but she said it would be like hitting cement from that height.

I have a vague recollection of playing with a toy on the floor of what must have been a Manhattan apartment while the adults were talking. The day was gray and muggy. I noticed a flash of lightning through the window, but when I pointed it out my father said it was probably a sea gull. Then there was a rumble of thunder.

Years later I found a novel that the old man confiscated, which contained a scene where this naked woman at a party was examining the floor on her hands and knees. When someone asked what she was doing, she said she was looking for her lost innocence. I always liked that line. I myself am dragging the river for my mind, because buying a .22 and drifting towards killing a President is conceivably symptomatic of a breakdown. Gunning one's way to celebrity: the shooting star blues.

6

Although the warehouse brings me down, it's a minor perk when the manager opens the extinct stock bin during the odd coffee break so that everyone can go for the damaged items, with the exception of Peter who always disappears down a back aisle.

As well as gathering stock, I stuff books into boxes which I've folded and taped together, packing them with tissue paper and cutting down the sides with a knife. After that, I number them in black crayon and tape on copies of the address, then get the packages weighed at shipping and receiving if there's a chance I'm making too big a box for the limit.

Before I finish taping one box up properly and signing my name to it, I give it back to the older Italian woman who'd filled the order, so that she can get it weighed. She assumes that I was planning on mailing it like that, and rolls her wagon straight to Walter, who marches down and accuses me of sending off books with insufficient padding. I argue with him since I hadn't signed off on the job, and say that the real problem is an old lady looking to cause trouble.

He pulls my boxes out of shipping and receiving while muttering to himself. After ripping a few open he decides that one of the cartons is packed too casually in the sense that I could have stuffed it tighter and cut down the sides by another inch or so to save maybe 15 cents on freight. In each instance there was enough padding to protect the stock, that being the crime of which I was accused, so he's obliged to let me off the hook but tries to justify the excitement by mumbling about my carelessness as he waddles back up the aisle.

The next day when Peter's back from sick leave, I give him two weeks notice. He in turn informs Walter, who tells him to remove me from the packing table. Peter subsequently approaches me in his confidential manner and asks what happened in his absence. When I explain the situation he says he doesn't want to lose me, and intends to complain about this injustice. Then, despite my protests, he goes off to see the warehouse manager.

Walter's predictably angered and stomps back with my supervisor in his wake, telling me he wants to discuss something in private. The three of us go down an empty aisle, where he demands to hear my version of events and argues that I was packing the boxes incorrectly. The upshot is that I'm to finish my employment in shipping and receiving.

Walter then follows me over there and proceeds to lambaste me in front of everybody, saying that he doesn't want to hear me accusing anyone of being like, a rat. I turn around and tell him that maybe the old bag *is* a problem. The shocked look on his face isn't bad. When he warns me not to push him any further, I tell him that he's scaring me to death, and he orders me to bugger off, to get my things and bugger off. I counter that he can't fire me because I already quit. This seems to fry his brain, but then he says that he'll give me a mop and pail and have me clean the washrooms until I leave, so I tell him to keep his fuck-ass job.

After collecting my coffee mug from the cloakroom, I start to fill in my hours on the clipboard hanging by his desk. He says not to bother, he'll do it, but I tell him not to concern himself. I then decide to clarify something about my health insurance with the bookkeeper, but when Walter sees me opening the door that leads to the office, he yells, "You're not allowed in there!" I ignore him and continue down the hallway while he runs after me on his fat legs, red-faced, eyes bugged out. When he catches up to me he loses some of his self-assurance without any other staff around. "Well, you can't talk to her anyway because nobody in there's come to work yet."

I look at my watch and realize it's only seven forty-five, so I turn to walk back into the warehouse.

"Boy," he says, "you're a great guy, aren't you?"

"At least I gave *you* two weeks notice."

I step out into the world wondering if I should ask for severance pay or just go straight for unemployment insurance. The way things ended isn't exactly clear-cut.

In the Isabella a pigeon feather alights on my toothbrush, which is lying before the bathroom window. Cockroaches wander my table while fire engines roar by outside. I notice a speck in my peripheral vision and take off my reading glasses to discover a tiny spider dangling from a web hitched to the wire frames. Pushing out my chair, I gently carry the creature across the room lest it drop from its thread, then open the door and lower my invader onto an empty gin bottle in the hall garbage can.

Five minutes later I'm distracted from my book again when two disheartened lovers run down the staircase and out onto the sidewalk below, where the man yells, "I hope you die in the street!"

Picking up a shirt from my closet floor, I discover writing on the bottom of the pink door: "If Only The Love Of My Life Was Here." I reflect on the human beings who have drifted through my room and wonder if their whereabouts might not be traced through the density of fingerprints around the switch.

Each rectangle of light in the twenty-eight storey high-rise across the street represents humanity living more expensively than I. Even if the St. Jamestown buildings are dirty or dangerous, they're still a step above a low-rent room in a rock and roll hotel. Who are those tenants? Where do they come from? What job titles do they give census takers? I often have the same questions when I'm on a train or segment of over-ground subway track and we're passing houses, thousands of them, row by row, street by street, into infinity. If one could only take a camera and follow everyone to work, to see who they are and what identities they assume in their jobs.

All the histories out there mystify me. When I see the outlines of countless men and women in their cars at night, I find it incredible that the same gamut of emotions exist in each of those heads. It's just a matter of degree, circumstance and behaviour.

And whether they dropped out of school or graduated from university, whether they are religious or criminally-inclined, whatever their stations in life, they leave behind feces like everything else on the face of the earth that walks, crawls, slithers, swims or flies. Yet again, everyone, of course, is unique.

Another thing I wonder about is how music evokes emotion. Is there something in our neurological make-up which responds to the predictable patterns of songs? We can anticipate the next note as if melodies fit a design on graph paper set in the brain, the structure of each hit having been drawn on a transparency to conform to the original, not unlike a number of locks matching one master key. And the way the contours of a song which has no apparent distinction will rise as if in high relief to hook you after you hear it a number of times. As there are only so many notes on the scale it seems mathematical that the possible variations for catchy arrangements are limited, and one can therefore understand why composers sometimes borrow from existing tunes.

It occurred to me at some point that all is not necessarily lost when you're on the bottom. The world will stare to see if your guts fall out, since the true measure of a man lies not in his downfall but in his recovery, i.e., Richard Nixon who departed politics blubbering that the press wouldn't have him to kick around anymore, then returned years later with his anti-Communist image revamped to win the Presidency and make significant advances in the field of foreign policy, especially with Red China. Though he left office on the verge of impeachment over Watergate, he didn't kill himself but kept a low profile, sparring lightly with the press and occasionally offering political insights. Rumours are circulating of a possible ambassadorial position. He'll probably end up writing a syndicated newspaper column or books on foreign policy, if he hasn't already. While Japan considers it honourable to commit hara-kiri when disgraced, America likes a man who rises above such odds.

I take the Glen Road exit from the subway station and walk west along Howard on my way home one night. The full moon, grazed by a jet trail, appears between two buildings and then vanishes. I stop and go back to observe this streak in the lunar aura which resembles the web crossing my light fixture: a striking geometry of line and circle. Continuing, I walk at a pace commensurate to that of a distant aircraft before hearing a disturbance.

On the west side of Sherbourne, across the intersection, a young Jamaican woman is shouting. "You afraid of pussy, mon? You *cocksucker*!"

She's wearing a long wig, a miniskirt, fishnet stockings. I don't know who she's talking to until I cross over and start walking south behind her. She throws a bottle at a black dude down the street. "Fuckin' *faggot*!"

He glances over his shoulder when it shatters.

She stops to confer with a white woman. I pause and ask if she's all right.

"No, he ripped me off!"

"Do you know him?"

"He's a pimp! Are you going to do somet'ing?"

The man, meanwhile, disappears down an apartment roadway leading into the ghettoized concentration of buildings along Bleecker.

She puts her hand on her hip. "Are you a cop or are you just talkin'?"

The other prostitute starts to drift away. "I just got out of jail, Shakura. I really don't want any more shit."

Well, I guess I'm just talking, but when she puts it like that, I don't really like to admit it. "I'm not the police," I say, "but I'll see what I can do."

And off I go with her behind me. I haven't gone thirty feet, however, when a car pulls over to the curb beside her. The woman discusses something with the driver through the passenger window. Then, turning to me, she shouts, "Forget it, he's gone. But thanks!" She gets in, and they drive away.

In the Isabella I decide to stop for a drink before continuing up to my room. There are three bars: the Lower East Side downstairs where punk acts play, the aforementioned Cameo blues lounge on the upper level, and a room I often hang out in off the main floor lobby with no cover, and a jukebox that focuses on blues, older R&B, roots rock and rockabilly.

Tonight it's fairly full. I end up in a conversation at the bar with a potbellied biker from Norfolk, Virginia. Sometimes I soak up local colour like a sponge. He tells me that he spent four years in the U.S. Navy and appeared in a number of motorcycle gang movies. "They know I'm a madman on my chopper, which'll go a hundred and thirty-eight miles an hour in eight seconds flat," he says, tugging the brim of his Harley-Davison cap. "I've driven through store windows and straight off cliffs."

He shows me a ring on one hammy fist. "See the 'double strike' symbol? That identifies the owner as an elite member of a club who has killed at least eleven people. The police consider such a person a terrorist, and once shot a man to death on the Peace Bridge to the States as soon as they recognized it – no questions asked. Anybody sees you wearing this ring and knows you haven't earned it, they'll fucking cut off your hand with a chain saw."

I drink some beer. "So you've killed at least eleven people."

He gives me a wily look. "Now, I'm not saying I killed anybody. All I'm saying is that I'm not afraid to wear it."

7

Another night I manage to talk up a fine looking black stripper at the Warwick who agrees to meet me after the show. Her name is Verna, or so she tells me: a tall, slender woman in her early twenties, with close-cropped hair and an aquiline nose that may have once been broken.

She emerges from the dressing room swinging her hips, a white purse over her shoulder. There are sequins down the sides of her jeans. Bars are closing by this time, and the only other place in the immediate neighbourhood is another strip joint about a block east between Jarvis and Sherbourne. Well, there's also George's Spaghetti House, but she says she doesn't like jazz, especially flute, so it looks like I'm just seeing her home.

A little later as we cross a small park a few blocks east of the Summerhill subway station, I draw her to me and give her a kiss. She lingers but then breaks away in the semi-darkness with a throaty laugh. Someone's walking a dog further up the path towards what seems to be the hillside of a larger, adjoining park. I don't really know the area, but I think we're in a section of what might be termed Upper Rosedale, a contrast to the inner city we'd recently left. North of Bloor, through a ravine or two, and you're in a different world.

She lives in a stately home with a verandah and bay windows. Her room is the first door to the left inside the front hall. A tabby cat drops off a chair, stretches, and pads over when we come in. I look at the coloured bottles arranged along the mantelpiece above a nonfunctional fireplace, on either side of which hang two fairly primitive-looking oil paintings. "Did you do those?"

"Uh huh," she says, taking off her earrings.

"They're good. Is that supposed to be . . . Jesus?"

She laughs, turning a little shy. "Yeah, from when I was younger."

"What about the other one, the self-portrait? Who's the guy?"

"Oh, just someone I thought I was once in love with."

A maroon batik of a butterfly is tacked on another wall. There are some plants beside the small stereo on the dresser in front of her window. She has a wardrobe with mirrored doors, shelves littered with cosmetics, a small TV.

We talk some more, she shows me some poetry and a few photos, alternately feigning modesty and being passionate, even slightly aggressive, when we start to kiss. I'm enjoying her full lips and the play of her tongue, and fondle her breasts through her top as I encourage her to undo my belt.

I stand to assist her. Verna frees my erect prick and sends a charge through me as she puts her hand around it, looking up sort of questioningly as she leans forward and kisses the head, and then sticks out a pink tongue and gives the underside a lick. When I touch her scalp, feeling the tight frizzy curls, she takes much of my cock into her mouth and begins to suck me up and down. Managing to unclasp and shift her bra, I toy with her hardened nipples as she caresses my balls and seems to lose herself.

I don't want to come yet though, and pull away to help undress her, and then myself. When we're naked on the bed I gently suck her pert tits and slide my hand down her abdomen to her bristly mons, touching the thick lips underneath, fingering her, caressing her clitoris. She is warm and wet inside. After shifting position I spread her legs and push them way back to expose her bum and the lushness of her vagina, which is as exotic as a jungle orchid within that dark outer labia. I open her pussy further and give her an exploratory lick, tonguing her deeply and lightly flicking her clit. I get more excited myself as she moans and squirms around while I eat her. Playing with her nipples or fingering her ass, I focus on the bud. Unsheathed, it is distended and pink.

Although God, so to speak, has created the act of defecation to make humanity humble and force us to realize that we are of the earth (the greatest man while sitting on the toilet being the sum total of his shit), women aren't equally reduced as their fundaments are borne with a certain gracefulness and can be considered *objets d'art*. The female anus is a source of fascination and surpasses mere digestion to become analogous with any black hole in space. We cheat Mother Nature by finding inspiration in this humble orifice, and undermine her reproductive course. I thank the creator or whatever for women who allow me to view beauty in humankind.

After she rocks her wild way into orgasm, Verna and I seem to share a rare intimacy as I slowly slide the length of my rod into her sweet cunt.

Afterwards, however, she's moody. "It's all a game," she says, striking a match.

"What is?"

"Everything. When I met you in the bar tonight I thought you were passive, but I can see I was wrong. You're dominant like I am. A relationship would never work unless one of us cracked, and baby, it wouldn't be me." Apparently my silence antagonizes her. "Well, why don't you say something? Doesn't it bother you?"

I guess I've misjudged her as well. It appears she's a bit crazy. "Listen, what do I care? One might say I got what I came here for, so if I walk out the door right now, I'm no further behind." I prop myself on my elbow. "Are you asking me to leave, or what?"

Verna takes a drag and turns away to exhale, candlelight silhouetting her striking profile. "No, I still want you to be my lover. Don't ever fall for me, though. What we have here's just a physical thing."

We're walking downtown along Yonge Street the next afternoon when she wants to see a movie or something but can't decide, and ends up criticizing me for not assuming the lead and taking control of the situation. Well, I had been in a good mood, and resent not only the implied insult but her contradictory expectations.

Later on her bed we seem to forget our hostilities and are oblivious to murder, plague, the acid rain drumming against the window. During a naked conversation afterwards, however, Verna mistakenly thinks that I'm laughing at her when I find something she says amusing, and demands that I stop so authoritatively that I can't. She comes off the mattress like she was shot from a cannon and tries to wallop me. I have to wrestle with this madwoman and manage to push her back onto the bed, but she bounces right back up, pulling my hair and kicking me, before breaking away to grab her acoustic guitar from behind the door. She swings it by the neck as she spins around towards me, and it slices through the air by my head as I duck and go for her, getting her down on the bed again and pinning her beneath the blanket. She shouts at me to fuck off and get out of her place. I let her up, and she pulls on her dressing gown, telling me that she's going to get the super to throw me onto the street before she stalks from the room.

When Verna returns she looks surprised to see me getting ready to hit the road, evidently having only been to the washroom. "I was just *kidding* about you leaving," she says, laughing softly, and lets her gown fall to the floor as she draws me back to the bed to continue our twisted passion.

8

I was watching our black and white TV late one sunny afternoon when my father returned from work. For some reason he paused in the living room doorway, and said, "I've taught you everything you know."

At four and a half I'd seen something of life, and conjured the most fundamental fact for which he couldn't possibly take credit: "Even that bees make honey?"

"Yes."

On the very first day of kindergarten I was standing outside school waiting for class to begin, when a chunky red-haired boy with freckles approached me. "Let's race," he said. "I bet I can run faster than you."

"No, I don't feel like it."

My defeatist attitude dates back to the embryo.

I went to school every day from nine o'clock until noon. While Bobby's mother watched *The Edge Of Night*, chain-smoking Rothman's and typing envelopes at her card table, he and I played outside, sometimes digging between the houses.

One afternoon while he was pissing against the wall, she peered around the corner with an expression of such horror and disgust that I was frightened. How could she have heard his trickle through the brick, above the television and clatter of keys?

"I *thought* so!" she shrieked. "You little *pigs!*"

"*I* didn't do it!" I cried.

Another time, Bobby threw some dirt on me and I chased him into his living room with a sand pail, pitching the contents all over him and the sofa. I dashed home while she was screaming.

One Saturday we were playing between his couch and picture window with Doug and his older sister, Helen, when Bobby suggested telling jokes. She began by asking why the man threw his clock out the window.

"Because it was old," I answered, linear perceptions intact.

"No!" the others chimed in unison. "Because he wanted to see time fly!"

I was not only unfamiliar with the expression but the concept of riddles in general, and only pretended to understand. Somewhat disconcerting, considering that I was a year older than the other boys.

My kindergarten teacher continued this wordplay. If she asked, "Who left this mitten on the floor?" and someone answered, "Not me, Miss Perkins," she'd retort, "I didn't ask who *didn't* leave it on the floor, I asked who *did*."

"Who has to go to the washroom?"

"I don't, Miss Perkins!"

"I didn't ask who *didn't* have to use it, I asked who *did*."

Fuck off.

My first gesture of conscious rebellion took place at school on visiting day. Bobby and Doug were registered for next year's kindergarten class, and were sitting with their mothers in the designated chairs. We were skipping around the room when the teacher called out, "If you've got friends who are here with us today, give them a wave and let us dispense with all further talking."

No doubt I've magnified my action to heroic status over the years by extending the time between this command and the moment when I chose to wave—and the petulance with which I did so—but nonetheless, I ignored the request and continued skipping while all the little hands fluttered, and then shot up my own in spectacular fashion after the others had disappeared from the air. Perhaps the difference between my hand and everyone else's was so slight that it was barely noteworthy, although it is possible that my memory has been faithful and I truly was a child of character.

A girl with whom I was enamoured in grade one was appointed classroom monitor to check everyone's desks for neatness. I assumed that she reciprocated the unspoken love I nurtured for her and was rather jumpy as she came down my aisle. It was an overcast spring morning and the clock ticked very loudly. It seemed that she returned my smile as she approached.

I pushed out my chair and folded my hands in my lap like a perfect gentleman while she did her inspection, then felt utterly betrayed when she straightened up and announced that my desk was untidy. It so happened that I was the only member of the class to have outraged authority, and was informed in an austere tone that I would be staying after school for a week.

Not knowing what this entailed, I figured I wouldn't be allowed home until next Monday, and envisioned sleeping beneath my desk while caretakers piled chairs and swept sawdust along the floor.

On another occasion the teacher said that she wanted us to draw colourful pictures for a little contest, and she'd tack the best one on the bulletin board. Following these criteria, I created a boy with an orange complexion and rainbow clothes beneath an imaginatively tinted sky and bright red sun, using every crayon at my disposal. Now, this same secret love who ratted on me won the competition with a lousy picture of a girl in a modest blue dress within a conservative colour scheme that required four or five stinking crayons, tops. Yes, it was good, but it wasn't as colourful as mine—which I understood to be of prime importance. And my fucking desk *was* tidy.

This apple of my eye had an older brother who was the terror of my life from grades one to four. He was two years older than I and went to junior high after that. I remember the incident that first brought him into my radius: I was minding my own business in the school yard one recess period when I suddenly found myself surrounded by a circle of girls, among whom was his sister, all linking their hands to secure me in their mighty fortress. I was tickled to be the centre of their attention. When some of my friends thoughtfully suggested that I break through the ranks or punch one of them in the nose, her brother, appearing out of nowhere, said he'd beat me up if I tried it.

I must have complained about his continuing harassment, because I was taken from class by the teacher evidently wishing to judge my story against his, and was mortified to confront him in the hall.

"Is this the boy who's been bothering you?"

"Yes," I managed.

"Well, he's got a gang that comes after me," he countered. "I just pay him back when he's alone, that's all."

His logic quite unearthed me, for I had only the vaguest conception that I was a member of a gang or that this gang had annoyed him. Even if some of my six-year-old friends were in conflict with this bully, they hardly constituted a group with a collective intelligence. I felt a strange pride in being thus accused, however, for it sounded terribly prestigious. In fact, I was so overwhelmed that I couldn't come up with an answer.

Twenty minutes later I was feeling embarrassed by my failure to justify the trouble the teacher had taken on my behalf. I put down my pencil and stood up while the class worked quietly, then walked along the aisle by the windows to her desk where I asked a troubling question to impress upon her the depths of my sensitivity: "Is it all right if I fold my hands like this instead of like this when we say our morning prayer?"

"That's fine," she said, hardly noting my demonstration. I returned to my seat, slightly unsatisfied with our brief spiritual communion.

If by some chance I'm bringing tears to your eyes, one day I crept downstairs in a vindictive spirit after having been banished to my room, and stuck a pen in my inflatable Popeye punching bag.

9

Most afternoons or evenings when she isn't working, I take the subway to Verna Johnson's neighbourhood and cross the small park to her house on Summerhill Gardens, where we ball and talk, listen to music, watch TV. Afterwards, my foxy woman with her funky broken nose and flashing eyes and short woolly hair and lean body with legs up to here might wrestle the honky away from the door, and drag me back to the bed. She's emotionally intemperate, the purveyor of psychological mazes—some of which may be due, I'm guessing, to the insecurity of growing up in orphanages and foster homes. She says that when she was thirteen she hated the woman in charge of her place so much that she soaped the stairs, hoping she'd break her neck.

Verna reinvented herself in a way by unofficially changing her name from Lindsay when she got into her first band. She says she's essentially a singer, and only started dancing five or six months earlier to make some money after the last group broke up. That seems to be true enough, judging from her ex-guitarist who sometimes drops by to visit, a seemingly catatonic redhead with a missing tooth. She also hangs out with a few of her neighbours, particularly two white women in the next house who survive on welfare, minor drug dealing and mother's allowance. One of them has a three-year-old daughter whose father's working in a mine in northern Manitoba.

Occasionally Verna comes down to the hotel. In our moments of repose we drink wine from plastic cups and listen to the radio while she taps her ashes into an empty pop can. Lying on her stomach beside me one day, she says, "You know, our relationship isn't only physical anymore."

"What do you mean?"

"Let's face it, we've become more than just lovers. We've gone out with your friends, I fix you dinner . . ."

"I thought you gave me a speech about not getting involved."

She gives me a coy smile. "I only said that so you'd show some emotion. You seemed so fucking bored it was making me crazy."

"Really. Well, I guess things have changed. We should probably take it easy, though, the way everything's always so up and down."

Verna turns and leans on her elbow. "That's just... the circumstances."

Later, when I come out of the washroom, she's propping the window higher with a book. From room No. 53 we're above much of the grit and dust off the street, though I usually find the traffic and construction noise distracting, and keep the curtains half-drawn against the heat once the sun starts beating down. "So, how come your group broke up?"

She settles into another position. "Oh, politics . . . Everybody in a band always thinks they should be going to bed with a woman singer. Male egos, and all that shit. It's the same with other women in bands I've talked to. You've got to work through so much garbage just to play music."

"You can't let that stop you, though. Just tell them straight off next time."

"I know . . ."

" I like your voice. It's got a rough edge to it. You ought to sing me a song sometime." I reach for my throwaway party cup. "Have you ever done anything flashy when you're dancing? I saw a stripper once who somehow lit matches on the ends of her nipples. I think she was called Hot Tamale."

Verna laughs and shakes her head. "You're a degenerate. That's why you're such a good lover: you've got no morals."

"Hey, I've got morals."

"I never do any of that stuff. I'll use props like that long wig I have, but I never do any of that other bullshit. I used to wear that wig in the band, too."

"Does it ever get in the way when you're stripping?"

She smiles. "No, I've never danced in the kind of place where you really had to fuck the stage."

Since we've been spending so much time together, I've been wondering about her background. She's on the pill and says she's never had the clap or anything, so I haven't used condoms. After a moment, I say, "There are a lot of hookers where you work. Do you know any of them, or ever hang out together at all?"

"No." She takes a sip of wine. "Some of the other girls are friends with them, but I don't really know them. I don't socialize in that place much."

"What about the other dancers? Do they ever hook on the side?"

"I don't know what they do. Dancing is completely different from prostitution. If they ever do that, it's their business, but I'd never sell myself if that's what you're wondering. Men like to buy me things anyway, without any promise of sex. Like my blouse, the one I was wearing yesterday? And my boots over there. I'd never degrade myself like that."

"I'm not suggesting you would. And I don't know if it's such a big deal anyway. A friend and myself bought a couple of them there a while ago—"

"What, prostitutes? Where I work?"

"A long time ago. I don't even remember what they look like."

Verna sits up and reaches for her cigarettes on the window sill. "Don't you know that every time a woman does that, a piece of her dies? She loses all self-respect, but you don't care, do you?"

"You're being a little dramatic. Why are they in the business?"

"Listen, in the absence of love or understanding or anything that makes people succeed or want to go on, a lot of them become hookers, and it's sad. It's *pathetic*."

"Well, I agree it's mostly psychological. I had this Marxist professor once who claimed that prostitution was the result of not having enough money in a capitalistic society. Out-of-date communist propaganda. I argued how that was a small factor in this

day and age, it was just a matter of making more money an easier way, and that hookers usually fit some kind of personality profile. More so anyway than just being poor."

"You're right," Verna says, getting off the bed. Naked, she
brandishes a smoke with her arm tucked under an elbow. "You
don't know how many of the girls I grew up with ended up prostitutes. When I was sixteen I had a girlfriend in the home whose
father was a drunk and couldn't take care of her. She got pregnant
and went back to live with him, and one night when she was out
he found her baby smothered. Crib death or something. Without
love or instruction, all feelings turn to hate or anger. Every emotion. Can you *imagine* that? She's selling herself on the street right
now."

I don't rise to it. "Okay, but in the immediate situation I think
it's the customer who's the sad case. The fact that he's paying for
it puts him in the degraded position."

"It tears them *up* inside!"

"Yeah, well . . ." I push the pillow against the wall and sit up.
"I'm not even sure it's that psychological anymore, considering
today's morality. Prostitution doesn't have the same shock value. It
just seems like an easier way to make money if you're attractive
enough and you can handle it. The women we were with weren't
in bad shape. It was just a job they were bored with."

"Were they tough or did they just act tough? A girl's wom-
anhood is her most valuable possession. The ones who sell themselves are very fucked up, and you just add to their problems by
encouraging them. All they can do is stay numb so they're not
bought out completely. That's what it means to be up for sale."

10

The publisher agrees to give me a couple of week's severance pay. Before I can collect unemployment insurance an old application I'd had with the post office gets me into the South-Eastern plant, one of the largest in the country. It's located in a district of low-income housing and auto wrecking yards off the lake shore, not far from a sewage treatment facility.

You show your photo ID to the guard when you go in, then pass the security room where a wall of screens displays areas of the building being monitored by cameras inside clouded domes. This affords Management a psychological edge over employees unable to tell where the lenses are pointing. Theoretically, everyone is under constant surveillance. After another set of doors at the far end of the lobby, you enter ten acres of noise.

I'm a part-time clerk (POL 4, Mail Prep, shift No. 3 on the mezzanine) and work evenings between six and eleven at a number of jobs: pre-culls, bag induction, traying stations, CFCs, the face-up table, cancelling machines, a/o recycle.

Occasionally I replace a mail handler on one of the bag shake-outs, hand-cancel, sort mail in ABC, Short And Long, or Oversize. Soon there will be training to learn how to send letters and small parcels by postal codes in the GDS and A/O Keying sections, respectively.

Verna, meanwhile, is being more emotional, less confrontational. I find that I'm getting involved with her but don't completely trust her, and try to remain invulnerable. Well, all right, I do tell her I love her when she asks me during a weak moment while we're having sex, which is the beginning of a pattern where she manages to draw this kind of an admission whenever I'm on the verge of coming. I mean, if I said it once I might as well say it again, and why spoil the moment when she herself is being confessional, and roughly speaking, the conflicting emotions I feel for her might constitute a kind of love.

But how easily such intertwining unravels. When I'm least expecting it, she informs me that she's attracted to a friend of mine and that she'd like to go to bed with him. She can tell he likes her too, and doesn't want to be held responsible for anything that might happen if she's drinking and I'm not around. I tell her that she'll be sorry if she does anything to dishonour me.

Subtle heat occurs between people all the time, but since there's no advantage in alienating one's lover by confessing it, I assume this is just another power play. Whether she's only trying to make me jealous or she wants to hurt me, I am, to say the least, wary.

A few days later, Verna asks whether I mind if she goes out drinking with her two neighbours on one of her nights off, and I tell her to enjoy herself, flattered in a way that she sought my approval.

Shortly after I get to her place the next afternoon, we're sitting on the bed talking when I ask her about her evening. She hedges with a nervous laugh. "Well, we saw a band at Larry's Hideaway . . ."

I stroke her cat. "How were they?"

"All right. We got pretty drunk and met these guys . . ."

There's something elusive in her manner. A flicker of uncertainty, amusement, it's hard to tell. She seems to need prompting. "And?"

"Oh, we had a good time, that's all." When I don't say anything, she asks, "What would you do if something happened?"

"I don't know."

Verna looks at me solemnly for a few seconds, then says, "I have to tell you—I went to bed with one of them, but it wasn't my fault. We were all pissed and checked into a couple of rooms together. I was kind of sorry when I woke up this morning."

Well, it's a boot in the head, but I'm not sure how to react. Walking out the door like a kicked dog doesn't seem so good.

Verna doesn't look very remorseful. In fact she's smirking, and begins to provoke me. "So, what are you going to do?"

"I haven't decided."

"Are you mad, honey, or what?"

"Listen." I speak as calmly as possible. "I don't need you and you know that very well. I come here for a laugh because you like the attention. You're a fucking joke."

Verna was looking for a reaction so she should have expected it, but she appears to have been struck. I'm distrustful at first by the transformation. "I . . . thought you loved me," she says, her voice breaking. "You don't care about me at all. It's just what I was afraid of—you've been using me." She gets off the bed and goes over to a chair where she starts crying. "You've dominated me and I've got no identity anymore!"

I watch her bawl. Hardly anything she does makes sense to me. After a couple of minutes it does seem to be real, however, so I go over and crouch beside her. Under the circumstances I'm really not sure what I'm supposed to say to her, though. "Look, I love you, all right? I was just pissed off. What did you expect?"

"I don't believe you."

"I'm sorry. I didn't mean it." Reluctantly, I put my arm around her shoulder.

"I didn't go to bed with anyone," she says through her sobbing. "I just wanted to make you jealous." Sniffing and wiping her tears, she turns to me. "I want to have a baby with you."

"What?"

"Think of how *beautiful* it'd be."

It strikes a chord, but since she's half-mad and I've never pictured myself with children, the idea of raising one with a hellion like her catches me off guard. "Listen," I say, "maybe we should just try to preserve the relationship for now."

Despite her erratic vulnerability she's basically a tough chick who'll get pissed off with her cat if he approaches me first, which on some level may be understandable, but I can't help wondering how she'd react to a wailing baby that wasn't reciprocating her affection.

II

Verna's dancing at the lounge the following Saturday evening when I take a streetcar to Parkdale in the west end to visit Sean Cochrane for a get-together with some people. He lives over a submarine sandwich shop on Queen near Jameson Avenue.

I ring the buzzer of a door with peeling paint and climb some stairs, then wait in a dreary hallway while he slides the bolts and peers at me through the crack. He closes it again and unfastens the chain.

"Owe people money?"

"Just precautious," he says as I go in. His blondish hair is combed back and hangs to his shoulders, and he's wearing a sleeveless T-shirt with the Stones logo. Nobody has arrived yet.

It would have been nice if Verna had been able to join me, but aside from the work roster she has her theories about drugs, certainly narcotics or anything involving needles. Even if she adjusted her perspective in this regard for the sake of a party, however, I'm not sure that I'd want to be a negative influence. I've turned a girlfriend or two on in the past without any complications, but she's managing to keep her head above water in an environment rife with prostitution as it is, without exposing her to additional trouble. Maybe she'd be fine without partaking herself, maybe not. Hell, I'm not sure I'd even know how to find a vein on a black girl.

In the narrow kitchen I tear open my beer carton and put some bottles in the refrigerator, then go into the living room and sit down on a ratty sofa. Cochrane comes in with a teaspoon, glass, and a plastic bag filled with white powder.

"I'll go set up your hit," he says.

After a few minutes he reappears and pulls a gun from his shoulder holster, aiming it at my head and then levelling it at the window. "If anybody tries to rip me off, they'll think twice when they see this." Reholstering it, he says, "Your hit's ready in the can." His track marks are multiplying.

I take another drink and roll up my sleeve. Withdrawing a syringe from my pocket, I remove its plastic top as I walk to the bathroom. The crystal meth sits in a bent teaspoon beside a glass of water on the toilet tank. I draw some water into the needle, flushing it out in the sink, then suck up some more and slowly squirt it out until I have twenty-five units left, which I empty into the spoon. Taking the top, I crush the granules and stir them up until a clear solution is formed.

I place a bit of cotton in the mixture and lay the needle point on it, absorbing all the liquid, then hold the syringe to the light and gently flick it with my finger to encourage the trapped air upwards. The plunger is pushed in until a tiny droplet appears at the point.

I lie the implement against the glass and take off my belt. Wrapping it around my left biceps, I pull it tight while pumping my arm with my hand clenched, then grip it between my teeth and rest one foot on the toilet. I pick up the syringe and lay it almost flat along the underside of my forearm, gently inserting it into the bluish vein in the crook of my elbow. Slowly drawing back the plunger so blood flows into the tube, I push it in with the belt relaxed, pull it out, then push it in once more to utilize any remnants and check for air bubbles, making sure the point didn't slip.

I sit on the toilet lid as the power overwhelms me. I feel fucking-A, although it doesn't seem as intense as it did the first time, nine years earlier. The theory is that the outlaw labs no longer had access to a particular chemical. I remember thinking that the rush was comparable to a sexual climax, and talked for what seemed like hours in a methodical stream when there was no hope for food or sleep. Weed heightens the senses while speed anaesthetizes. Coming down back then was even worse than now, but we must remember the good times. There was such a driving sense of euphoria that I'd get depressed just foreseeing the end of a party.

I wipe the droplet of blood from my arm with a tissue, and after a few minutes stand up and put on my belt. Drawing some water from the glass into the syringe, I squirt it in the sink and watch it run down the drain with a pinkish hue. I then put the lid on and toss the bloody paper and cotton into the toilet before dumping out the water, and click off the light.

In the living room I hand him a twenty. "Not bad."

"It's the best I've had in a while," he says.

I can remember when three hits cost five dollars. Speed creates a pleasurable sense of calm excitement, and therein lies the paradox as illustrated by the person who drinks tea or coffee for the caffeine's illusory relaxing effect, or the medicinal use of Ritalin—a central nervous system stimulant—to treat hyperactive children.

Cochrane goes out for cigarettes. I sit in an armchair and look through a couple of magazines. His apartment lacks a sense of personal decor in that the furniture seems haphazardly collected, probably second hand, and the posters are generic material that you'd find in framing stores or record albums, with the exception of one with a skull and crossbones he must have ripped off a medical clinic, that warns, "Speed Kills." Thin curtains flutter at the dirty window overlooking Queen Street.

When Cochrane returns he goes directly into the kitchen, then comes back out and walks over to me. "Have you been into my stash?"

I look up, surprised. "I don't even know where it is."

He turns and goes into the bathroom.

"You better lay off the meth," I call after him. "It's making you paranoid."

And it is, I guess. I remember him once telling me in a very considered, logical way how he suspected Don Waters of giving him up to the police. Waters, who we'd tried to visit in the detention centre, was a fairly hardened case of impeccable reputation who had been stabbed and hit with beer bottles, but I did know Cochrane better and generally respected his judgment. Indirectly, we went back a long way. I've got the face of an angel, however, and he obviously doesn't trust me either. Anyway, soon the party will be underway.

People step around Izzy, who's crashing out on Seconal and beer near a broken bottle. I sit on the sofa talking to Egbert Hahn, an accountant who continues to deal pot on the side, and his girlfriend, Suzie. Her long curly hair is cut in a shag, and her nail polish is sparkly. She has a tendency to discuss psychics and astrology, but she's so guileless and good-natured that you can't hold it against her. Making conversation, I ask what her philosophy is.

"About what?"

"Life and death."

She glances at her boyfriend who's looking at his beer. "Oh, I don't care about any afterlife. I mean, people are my life. Whenever I go anywhere I either die, or . . . Stop bullshitting me! I never know when you're serious. What I mean is, is that people are my life. When I die I'm just going to die."

"What about reincarnation?"

She laughs. "Well, okay, if you want to start talking about *that*—"

As if to change the subject, Egbert says, "I may have to stop dealing." When I ask him why, he takes a drink and leans forward with an arm on his knee. "I had this thirty pound sale the other day, right? I shouldn't have done it so close to home, I realize that now. As I was walking down the street to meet the guy, a car passed me going the opposite direction. It looked like an unmarked dick car, but that didn't bother me at the time. The courier pulls up at the corner and gives me the dope, and I pay him and then go to where the buyer's waiting. Afterwards I get dropped off a few blocks from my place and see the unmarked car that passed me earlier sitting on the corner of my street. I take a short cut home to avoid him, then see another car parked outside my house. Well, I go inside because he's seen me, and—"

"But you weren't carrying anything?"

"No, but they could plant something, take me down to the station . . ."

Egbert rubs his five o'clock shadow. He has pronounced features and a background of uncertain ethnicity. His eyes are inscrutable. With a practiced nonchalance, he usually manages to allude to these deals as an afterthought or matter of passing interest.

"Well," he continues slowly, "I had to meet somebody, so I leave by the back door while the car's still parked outside, and go to the library where he's supposed to pick me up. I pass the police station on the way and see the first car there in the lot, so I know he's a cop. I meet my friend, and I don't know if I was followed or if they were looking for me, or even if it's all in my mind, but it seems a hell of a coincidence that there are two marked cars behind us as we drive down the street. When I tell him what's going on, he's paranoid that they're going to tear out the seats looking for shit. We take the 401 to see if they're on our tail, and one cruiser disappears and the other one stays on our ass for a few miles before turning off."

"How much money did you make?"

"Four hundred and fifty bucks. Not bad for a couple of hours work."

"Well, ignoring the ten years off your life."

It's been over three years since I've seen Mike DeLurgio, a one-time dealer who supposedly made in excess of a hundred thousand dollars, some of which was used to put down payments on a couple of houses which were later condemned. He also ripped off a number of people and travelled to Jamaica with Izzy before he lost his mind.

This first became apparent when he threw away an expensive bag of junk while walking with some friends, thinking he was being followed, and shortly thereafter withdrew to his family's basement near Niagara Falls. He sat down there wrapped in a blanket and didn't much talk to anyone, wash or go outside, except to hit the liquor store or wander the streets at night. He also phoned somebody long distance, claiming to have slept with the guy's girlfriend through ESP.

DeLurgio then tried to drive out west but turned back at Sault Ste. Marie. After that he flew to Vancouver, where he later said he spent four days drunk on wine in his hotel room. When Izzy and Terri, DeLurgio's ex-girlfriend, dropped by around midnight on their way home from Buffalo, he was staring out the window for UFOs but was sufficiently cognizant to tell them, teary-eyed, that they couldn't possibly understand what had happened to him inside.

Now I've heard that his family has evicted him from the cellar, and the people with whom he's staying in town are distressed by his tendency to fall asleep in front of their TV with lit cigarettes. He has a passing resemblance to killer Charles Manson, and looks a little ragged, but despite the tangled hair and missing teeth doesn't strike me as noticeably altered. If anything, he seems more communicative, taking into account that he never much liked me.

When I ask how he's doing, DeLurgio mumbles that he's been fucked up, so we discuss it briefly and I broach the idea of professional help. Encountering no resistance, I then suggest that we try to check him into The Clarke Institute of Psychiatry later.

After I come back from the washroom, a woman named Lois appears from the crowded kitchen, steps over Izzy, and says hi as she takes a seat near me on a chair by the sofa.

"How are you?"

"Okay . . . Carol had trouble with her boyfriend about coming out tonight, but everything's all right now. He and Zane are the jealous types." Taking the purse from her shoulder, she pulls out some cigarettes.

"Is Zane your sugar daddy?"

Her hand flutters as she flicks her lighter. Clicking it shut, she exhales. "No, he's a Vagabond. You're behind the times."

"How's your daughter?"

"Oh, fine . . . She's three now. Her father's in jail with the rest of his biker friends."

Lois and I once went out, but it didn't go anywhere. Although her nerves seem a bit shot, she's looking pretty well given her history of speed and hepatitis. The yellow hue is gone and there's a sheen to her dark hair, a healthy broadness to her ass. After the doctor told her she had half a liver left and that the next bout might kill her, she'd re-contracted it at least twice.

She smiles faintly. "Did you know I got splashed up at Wasaga Beach last summer?"

"What?"

"Splashed. Gang-banged. I was with two Vagabonds and there was an argument over which one was going to fuck me, so the gang had a vote and everybody won. I didn't mind the first seven, but the next fifteen wore me out. My youngest sister took on twenty-eight of them and enjoyed it more."

"Isn't she only fourteen?"

"She just turned thirteen."

Sometime after twelve, I get a ride for DeLurgio. A few of us leave Cochrane's flat and walk to a car on Sorauren. Although his neighbourhood is generally known for crime, rooming houses, psychiatric outpatients, drugs and bottom-of-the-barrel prostitution, there's a strange sense of community along that strip of Queen. The side streets have trees and large, older homes.

We drive east to the Clarke at Spadina and College, opposite the blinking lights of the run-down Silver Dollar: a strip bar where James Earl Ray, the convicted assassin of Martin Luther King, used to hang out drinking after the shooting in 1968. He lived in an Ossington Avenue boarding house pretending to be a real estate salesman, before flying to London. I like the thought of this infamous white trash sitting incognito in a bar that I myself sometimes haunt over ten years later.

A sturdy-looking female doctor with graying hair and a stern demeanor meets us in the lobby. When I tell her that our friend would like to sign in for treatment, someone with us, a guy named McAuley, wants to be the one to explain the situation. He rambles inarticulately about DeLurgio's acid trips while she becomes increasingly impatient and our man paces the floor, smoking.

The doctor gathers that drugs are the problem and wants to admit him to the rehabilitation program. At this point I presume upon his privacy by charting his downfall to better illustrate his frame of mind, but McAuley interrupts and oversimplifies the situation by getting into the drug business again, and she seems determined to put him into the addiction wing.

"With all due respect," I say, "I don't believe that's the problem. He's not here to get off drugs. LSD was at most a catalyst for what could be a form of schizophrenia."

"Don't tell me my job," she snaps. Turning to DeLurgio, she asks, "What exactly do you think your problem is?"

"Fucked up," he mutters without looking at her.

"I won't admit him. We only accept people who want to be treated."

"If he could express himself properly he wouldn't be here in the first place," I say. "He's obviously signing in of his own free will."

"Don't tell me about psychiatry. This is for *me* to decide." She crosses her arms and stares at him. "Would you like to discuss your problems?"

DeLurgio, who's getting agitated, takes a drag and says, "Fucking bullshit."

The doctor looks back at me. "It's clear he doesn't want treatment. Perhaps you'd better leave."

Well, I've been drinking, I'm still speeding, and I don't like her attitude. "Not until another doctor looks at him."

She turns and walks away. I'm impressed that DeLurgio has the fortitude to withstand such public scrutiny, and almost feel grateful to him for placing his now-inconceivably fragile existence in my hands.

Ten minutes later the woman returns with an older male doctor and two security guards. When I begin to restate the case, however, DeLurgio suddenly runs for the door and disappears into the night.

12

The first woman I ever saw naked was Bobby's mother. I guess I was about seven. We went into his house one afternoon and noticed her in her bedroom at the top of the staircase, just inside the doorway at her dressing table. I stood there with my mouth open for a few seconds, taking in a side-view of her breasts and pubic hair until she saw us and shrieked for his father. We bolted outside.

Heavenly spirits intervened on my behalf one Sunday night after visiting my grandparents in the east end, when I jumped two or three steps from their cement path to the sidewalk and twisted my ankle. My mother said that the angels did this to me, for in my foolishness I might otherwise have continued into the street and been run over by a car.

As we filed out the door at the end of the day, I stepped from line and informed my grade two teacher with whom I was in love that I wished I could go home with her, but she politely kissed me off.

A girl in my class failed the year. When I asked her why, she bitterly explained that Mrs. H. once thought she was talking but it was somebody else. How early we learn to rationalize defeat.

I roller skated beside my father on my way to get a haircut, zooming ahead, retracing my ground and racing past him until we got to the shop. I was the only customer, and was consequently offered a choice of barbers. After I removed my skates, the elderly Anglo Saxon and three younger Italians were standing there smiling at me expectantly. Since they'd been equally nice to me in the past, I think I went straight to the closest one without agonizing over it.

On the way home my father inadvertently inflicted me with everlasting guilt by remarking that the old man was very hurt that I didn't pick him. Oh, how I've since wished that I'd scrambled into his chair instead, being so distinctive and obvious with his white hair and glasses, but perhaps I didn't want to appear prejudiced to the others, or patronizing in light of his age.

During my first real physical examination I was horrified when the doctor crouched to pull down my pants and underwear. Afterwards in the car I choked back tears while confessing my humiliation to Mother. At the next check-up when he got down and unzipped me, I compounded my self-consciousness with a boner.

Doug's family was at the cottage one summer when I suggested to Bobby that we open their garage and ride around on his sister's bicycle. Although we returned it unharmed before they came back, a neighbour apparently witnessed our mischief because the fat mother spoke to me about it later.

A family living down the street had always been suspect among us for a fragrance which arose from their property in the spring with the melting snow, the result of bad sewage or thawing excrement perhaps, since young Harry, a.k.a. Hairy Banana, liked to shit outdoors. I remember some kids, girls included, getting him to lie on the gravel driveway with his pants down so they could wedge stones into his ass crack.

His father worked for a potato chip company. Once, we opened the van parked in their driveway and riffled through the merchandise, grabbing as many bags as possible before fleeing up the street to my house. I remember looking back as I was running to the end of my yard and seeing the other kids behind me, chips flying in the wind.

That fall I invited all the boys who hung out in the same group at school to my birthday party, except for a guy named Eric, and tried not to think about this unkind omission since I had nothing in particular against him. A couple of months later when he did the same thing to me, I told him without any explanatory preamble that I'd just forgotten to invite him. He knew immediately what I was referring to, and answered that he'd just forgotten to invite me too. I didn't begrudge him his revenge, but only wished to acquit myself, seeing as how I'd obviously hurt him.

Craig, one of the older twins who lived next door, was always fighting with his brother. One morning I went over to Bobby's and found him passing a cigarette around to everyone in the tent out back. When I took a puff, he insulted my integrity by exclaiming, "Lane smoked it! Now he can't tell on us!" He instructed us to swallow toothpaste when we went home to avoid detection, but after doing so I proudly confessed to my mother anyway. She expressed the appropriate disapproval without making an issue of it.

On another occasion, Craig, myself, Doug, his older sister, and a couple of her friends were hanging out on a porch when Craig decided to leave, and labelled the girls "dick-weeds" on his way down the steps. This, he explained, was when weeds were growing out of your dick. He and young Doug went over to his house, but I elected to stay with the females. I suspected that remaining behind seemed less manly, but I found their company more interesting. Overall, my opinion probably hasn't changed. And I always preferred the less macho Archie comics to superheroes like Batman, but at least Archie and Reggie were trying to make it with girls instead of running around in tights with the likes of Robin.

Craig and his brother hid in a store until it closed, and spent the night eating candy and reading magazines. The police brought them home.

A year or so later he got leukemia. He told me how he pissed blood, then his hair fell out from chemotherapy. Although I was his neighbour, someone else in my class was called upon first to discuss daily news items, and reported the news of his death before I could.

Having seen so many TV shows where a bad man was waiting behind a door, I always pushed it against the wall when entering a room. My mother was evidently aware of my paranoia, because one day while I was tearing downstairs from the bathroom, she called out to explain that a hot water bottle was hanging up back there.

In trying to establish my identity in the hierarchy of school-boys, I compared myself with Tom Kennedy, another blond kid of slight stature. The first time I invited everyone back to my house, somebody complained about the distance, so I explained that we should probably run—it wasn't so far if you ran. Thinking this would sound plausible if Tom said it.

In November 1963, our grade three teacher came into the room and told us that President Kennedy had been assassinated. After a pause, somebody shouted to Tom that he better run home because his father was dead, and everyone laughed, including the old lady.

13

In October Verna hints that I should buy her an engagement ring. Aside from the fact that we haven't known one another very long, I tell her that I can't provide for her and any kid on what I earn, and that I'm thinking of heading out west for a few months to make some money in construction. She suggests we go together, but I explain that I'll be staying in camps which don't accommodate women, and that if we break up she'd be stranded in the middle of nowhere. She tells me to fuck myself and doesn't pay much attention when I suggest that maybe we can move in together when I get back. Not being immune to her voodoo, I don't want to burn all my bridges.

Shortly after that she checks into the hospital with tonsillitis. A week and a half after her recovery, Verna suggests that I use condoms until her next period, having realized from talking to the girls next door that things may not be that safe. She had been too sick to swallow anything in the hospital, including her birth control pills, and was under the impression that it wouldn't matter as long as she resumed taking them when she got out. So, in effect, we've been having sex without protection.

I start wearing prophylactics, but at one point the latex breaks while I'm fucking her from behind with my hands on her bum cheeks and her asshole winking at me, and I ejaculate deep inside her molten core while she moans into her pillow.

Son of Sam was a postal worker who supposedly took his instructions to kill people at random from a dog. The South-Eastern plant has its own league of mentally ill: Wanda in Short And Long yells obscenities while she works, and once spit in the face of a lame black mail handler and called him a nigger. Story has it that she's a former school teacher who lost her mind after seeing her family burn to death in a car crash. An old woman in a Nazi helmet is dismissed from ABC occasionally to take a bath, a male clerk in pigtails and make-up is sent home every once in a while for wearing a dress, and a psychotic who responds to orders but doesn't otherwise communicate with anyone was suspended and then transferred to Mail Prep for punching a pregnant woman.

Everyone has a history, or at least a life outside this part-time shift. On the traying station, my toothless partner Al tells me that he used to play professional hockey, owned a folk music coffee house, and while employed as a cameraman for the CBC, was possibly the first person in the country to learn of President Kennedy's assassination. It seems that he was visiting a friend at Associated Press that day when the bulletin clicked out of their Teletype machine. Since nobody was around, he tore it off and called his boss.

While we're talking, Al is hit by a rubber band. Brushing back his greasy pompadour, he sends a volley of elastics over the north side, then lifts his tray of mail onto the conveyor belt. "Even CBC got their international news from AP back then," he says, "so we scooped everybody."

Sarah received a commendation from the Canadian Film Institute for her work in a three-minute animated short, which was shown at a world festival. She's hoping to be hired by the National Film Board, and freelances on TV commercials.

Reuben's a high-strung jazz fusion guitarist with short curly hair, who once suffered an ulcer for which he had to be replenished with four pints of blood in twenty-four hours. His lung also collapsed in a restaurant.

Adrian from Vancouver is tall, angular and low-keyed. He takes a lot of courses, does volunteer work, writes the odd play for college radio stations and fringe festivals, and dresses in a pastiche of styles from silk to radical chic. His future seems plotted around trips abroad and the postal stations to which he can transfer across the country.

Jesus is a West Indian of Portuguese, African and Scottish descent who plays trumpet in funk and jazz groups. He's also an alcoholic who likes to put a six pack in his locker and drift downstairs intermittently between six and eleven every night to drink it. During our fifteen minute break we'll sometimes drive over to a bar (seven minutes to travel, eight minutes for beer), and while in A/O Keying where there's next to no supervision, we've left for up to half an hour to drink or snort coke.

Every shift is a bright, droning, fabulously mechanized hell. Burlap sacks of mail roll in from the docks and slide down the chutes of four bag induction stations, situated on a level above the mezzanine. As they continue up the belts, clerks pull each one into a large bucket, check the label, and press a button on the panel which flips it into a tray moving past on the track beneath.

First class mail is transported to the bag shake-outs where mail handlers empty the sacks onto conveyor belts, which disperse the envelopes and packages to the pre-culls below. Clerks there withdraw items inappropriate for the CFCs—large machines which cancel stamps at a rate of eight per second: packages are tossed down the a/o chutes, parcels are dumped in the cages behind them, while medical samples, stamped films, stray special deliveries and damaged goods are placed in black trays to be collected for hand cancelling, repairs or redirection. Bundles of metered letters, thick or oversized envelopes are sent down various belts to the traying stations to be stacked and dispatched elsewhere.

Remaining mail continues in a different direction to the CFCs. Finished letters are then sent to the GDS section downstairs for postal code processing. Rejected mail gets a second run through another CFC.

Everything unmachinable is relegated to the face-up table. Clerks sort through the pile, separating long and short envelopes and inserting them into slots on the edge, where a belt carries them along the sides to the end. They are then gathered and stacked on the ledges of two small cancelling machines. Letters too thick or large to be run through are put aside and packed in different trays behind the workers so their stamps can be voided by hand.

I'm working on a pre-cull one night with Janice, a lesbian who pickets strip bars, criticizes other women for wearing make-up, tries to persuade them to help her tear down pin-ups in the mechanics' cage, and claims she hates men because some authority figure molested her as a child.

For the hell of it I pass her a stupid postcard with a cartoon of a cowboy wearing a bra for earmuffs, which she takes in stride. Ten minutes later, however, she hands me another one with a sentimental illustration of a naked boy and girl warming themselves by a fire, and says, "If you want to get off, do it on something tasteful like this."

It seems an odd choice with which to lecture me, so I say, "This suggests that you view children as sex objects."

She tosses a package down the a/o chute. "They have a sexual life too. Remember how it was when you were young."

"That may be true, but we as adults aren't allowed to exploit their sexuality."

I don't think anymore about it until a week or two later . . .

Nicole is a diminutive left-wing, lower-case feminist who lives with her boyfriend and dresses like a street urchin in caps, undershirts, suspenders and patched pants. After her divorce she enrolled in Environmental Studies at university through which she hopes to get into law school. Since we often work together, we've become friends and she tells me about some of her classes—how she argued, for example, that the public take greater responsibility for the disposal of toxic waste. Clay deposits in southwestern Ontario were ideal for containing it with minimum risk of contamination, but people just wanted the shit buried up north where the resources couldn't handle it.

Janice, apparently mistaking Nicole for a sister, confided that her roommate sometimes has her former lover's ten-year-old daughter over, and that during one of the girl's visits the three of them took a shower together and soaped one another. The next time, they examined one another's genitals while the two explained masturbation and played with the girl's clitoris. Finally, whereby no academic distance was even pretended, Janice persuaded the prepubescent to suck her breasts. Nicole won't give me sufficient details to report them as she doesn't want to inform on anybody.

Verna has the night off. We end up in an argument over plans to go out after I change my mind about spending the whole evening in a bar to see a band. I suggest doing something else beforehand, like seeing a movie, but she's in no mood to compromise and starts shouting at me. I'm in the wrong for trying to modify the plan, but still: I feel that I've had enough of this shit. I tell her to have a good time. She looks up in amazement as I open her door to leave, and half-throws a chair across the room at me, yelling, "You fuck-! Don't *ever* come around here anymore!"

All right. *Fini.*

The next afternoon around 2:30, however, Verna comes down to the Isabella. After I answer the door I go back to the card table where I'm writing a letter. She looks around, then walks over to the unmade bed and sits down. "I was a bitch yesterday. I should probably apologize."

"There's no need to. It just proves once and for all that we can't get along."

Verna takes out a cigarette. She's looking good: thin black leather jacket, blue bandanna, lipstick, silver hoop earrings, a pink blouse, faded jeans, white pumps. She lights up and crosses her long legs. "Where's your ashtray?"

I find it under some papers and hand it to her.

She gives her cigarette a perfunctory flick, and says, "You know, you bring out the worst in me. I'm never so pissed off as I am around you."

"I know what you mean." I glance at her as I take a swallow from my can of Coke, then go back to the letter. I know I'm not being a good host.

Verna removes her jacket and kicks off her shoes. I keep writing, but it's hard to concentrate. The next time I look up, she's stepping out of her jeans. She laughs as our eyes meet.

"I wouldn't recommend you do that," I say. "You and I are done."

She pulls down her panties, undaunted. "You know you can't resist me. I can have you any time I want."

I return her smile. "Really, Verna, I'll have to throw you out of here if you continue." I watch her breasts spring into view as she takes off her blouse, then look back at the paper. "It's nothing personal, but I'm going to have to throw you stark naked out into the hall. You know I will."

She comes alongside me and brushes her dense pubic hair against my arm. Parting her legs, she rolls her hips and caresses my tattoos with her pussy, then bends down to touch my cheek with one dark, erect nipple. I stand up and take her hand. We move to the centre of the room until I veer her away from the bed. She tries to free herself, but I grab her about the waist and force her towards the door. She's strong but I somehow manage to hold her against the wall as I turn the knob, and then push her out into the corridor and slam the door, locking it. "Let me *in!*" she shouts, pounding with her fist.

"I warned you." I laugh, catching my breath. "You shouldn't underestimate a man with no morals."

I open up before anyone comes by. After the subsequent fight, our tempestuous relationship continues.

14

I don't bother bringing a shop steward with me to the counselling I have to attend with Dan Nyugen, general supervisor of Mail Prep, who was supposedly an officer in the South Vietnamese army and will be executed if he returns. Three pink slips for the same offense within a year are theoretical grounds for firing.

He gives me a carbon record of our meeting—

"Purpose of Interview: To discuss with you your unsafe act, namely shooting elastic band at another employee on 1980–21–10 at approx. 9:15 P.M. Your personal file will be involved. You have the right to be accompanied by a Union Rep. for the interview. You have the right to review your personal file prior to the interview.

"Narrative report: I, (D. Nguyen P.O. Sup. 5) formally interviewed Mr. L. Courtney, P/T POL 4 today 1980–23–10 for his unsafe act that was committed on the night 1980–21–10 at approximately 21:15 hrs. The employee did not request a Union Representative, nor did he want to review his personal file, although both were offered to him prior to the interview. At the beginning of the meeting the purpose of the interview was read and the employee was asked whether he had any explanation to offer regarding the above-mentioned irregularity on the night in question. The employee replied (quote): 'No, but there is something I would like to say.' I said: 'Go ahead.' Then the employee continued (quote): 'I apologize for my action on that night and it was carelessness on my part. I shall do my best to see that it will never happen again in the future.' I informed the employee that shooting elastic bands is an extremely unsafe act. It is not just distracting the attention of fellow employees, which has a negative impact on our productivity thus resulting in deterioration of the Postal service, but also it could cause permanent visual damage to another employee. This is contrary to Article 33:05 (a) and (b)—(then I read the article) as well as violation of Plant Rule #1 and #7.

"Now I am bringing the matter to your attention that shooting elastic bands in your work area cannot be tolerated by the S.C.L.P.P. management. Any repetition of the similar infraction on your part, you will be subject to further administrative actions. I hope this interview serves what it's intended for: that we will not have any similar actions from you in the future. A copy of this report will be placed on your personal file for a period as per the collective agreement. Further disciplinary action may arise as the result of this interview."

Given the four-hour option, a number of us leave the plant at ten o'clock as we usually do on Thursday night, and go over to the Orchard Park Tavern, a fairly rough bar near Greenwood Racetrack. Coloured lights flicker off a silver disco ball suspended above the dance floor, and the music is loud.

We're sitting at five or six tables. I take one of the ten milligram Valiums that I'd bought off a mail handler named Art, who steals them from the pharmaceutical company he works for during the day, and give one to Nicole and another to Rosa De Los Santos, a coworker from San Salvadore. She tells us that when she was recently arrested on a drunk and disorderly charge, they pissed her off at the station by making her take off her jewellery, so she stripped right down to her bra, panties and boots. This prompted one of the cops to ask for a date.

Art, wearing glasses and a standard-issue blue work shirt, strokes his moustache at the next table and describes a dog food eating contest at another east end bar, where the winner ate two cans of Dr. Ballard's. A shop steward, he carries his union briefcase everywhere in case somebody asks him to file a grievance or accompany them to a counselling. Despite an unassuming appearance he wears a "Fuck Authority" button, and took out his prick at a house party after the shift one night for anybody who would give him a quarter.

At some point I'm listening to Reuben tell me about the note clusters he's been generating through his Fender Stratocaster.

"I've been working on some experimental music," he says, leaning in over his draft. "Kind of an avant-garde fusion that might lend itself to video presentation. I'm thinking of trying to organize a concert at a gallery or some place other than a bar, since this stuff isn't too commercial. The music incorporates funny ideas and manipulates sound as opposed to being like a straight song format.

"We've got two guitars, a sax and a synthesizer. I want to get a drum machine too, I think. You program tracks into it, and that becomes your rhythmic basis. I don't know if I prefer it to a real drummer, but the source of sound are digital recordings of actual drums. It's exciting, and I guess it's economically advantageous. If anyone suggested five years ago that I'd be using a drum machine over a drummer, I'd have told them they were daft."

Reuben can be witty, even if his moods are on the odd side. One second he'll be giving you a worried sidelong look, and then in a manic groove be bouncing on the balls of his feet, his colour high, joking or going off on a rant. Or he'll shut right up and not talk to anybody. "The computer age scares me as much as anyone," he says, gesturing with his cigarette, "but there are a lot of people using the musical technique I'm fooling with—this experimental sound which extends the perimeters of the notes actually being played. Minimalism moves away from traditional roles and all the usual ways of playing things."

I take a second Valium with my third or fourth beer, and give another to the women. Nicole swallows hers with a swig of draft, and laughs—"Wanda was going around asking people if they masturbated today. What a *killer*." Despite her hairy armpits she exudes a spirited, bosomy femininity in her baseball cap and sleeveless T-shirt. I like the feathery earrings.

When she and Rosa slow dance, people aren't sure what to think. The locals in particular don't seem too happy about it. I stand on my chair and somberly announce: "I would like to make something perfectly clear. I do not now have, nor have I ever had . . . a venereal disease." There is some laughter. I sit down again.

Adrian takes a nearby seat. "Your eyes look like two piss holes in the snow."

"Where'd you get those white shoes?" Reuben asks him. "In a Portuguese store between the clay nativity scene and the bust of Elvis?"

Yes, the shoes are something. Adrian tends to be aloof, and speaks in a high register. He also moves with a catwalk slink and has cheekbones that cast shadows worthy of a fragrance ad, but he does seem to be as tormented by women as the rest of us. When I first met him his hair had been impossibly mod with bangs, but now he brushes it back and has traded in the glasses for contacts. He has an extensive knowledge of music, particularly British pop, and always seems to imply that he's got the inside track on new wave/punk clubs, poetry readings, anything Queen Street West. What had initially seemed pretentious is more or less proving legitimate however, and between his bouts of annoying pomposity I've since come to appreciate his unlikely moments of self-deprecation and absurdist humour.

Adrian asks if he told me about the woman he met at a booze can. "She was older and pretty drunk," he says. "I don't know what I was doing, because she wasn't my type at all, really, but I guess what interested me was that she said she used to live with one of the Mothers Of Invention." He laces his fingers in a sort of stretch. "I forget what instrument she said he played . . . As we were leaving, she threw her bottle into the crowd, and somebody came running out and punched *me* in the head as I was helping her down the stairs. I must have been kind of drunk too, because it didn't really hurt."

"Did you have sex with her?"

"No." He waves it off as he reaches for his glass. "She was too fat; I couldn't get into it. Her legs were . . . they were like *piano* legs. When we were fooling around her bed collapsed."

Although I don't remember the segue exactly, I say something to the effect that as far as danger goes, the closest I ever came to death was sitting through Andy Warhol's *Chelsea Girls*. He seems to like that so I get into some random philosophy, telling him, "I saw Sartre's philosophy on a rerun of *Leave It To Beaver* the other day. The kid gets caught letting a friend into the theatre by the back door, and his uncle punished him but didn't tell his parents. When Beaver thanked him, he explained that if you impressed upon a kid how bad he is often enough, he'll believe it and try to live up to the reputation.

"Well, that's Sartre's justification of Genet's behaviour, right? Genet was branded a criminal as a kid, and accepted it. So you can figure that either *Beaver*'s scriptwriter was a philosophy graduate, or else Sartre was rewriting homespun logic. And the most important thing," I say, trying to get it across without slurring, "is that Sartre was contradicting existentialism, because Genet, who he saw as the ultimate outsider, would have created his own morality independent of external judgments. Oh, and by the way, fucking Sartre's Marxism and existentialism cancel each other out. He should have either backed the state *or* the individual."

Or something close to that. "And speaking of communism . . . For all its objective toughness, it's afraid of sex. They crush individual freedom to benefit the majority, right? Well, much of any population's lonely or unhappily married or whatever, so for the sake of the unfulfilled, communists should institute rotation mating. You know, make beautiful people share the wealth too."

Then it's psychology. "But the biggest fucking joke is Freud's Oedipus Complex. One doesn't sleep with one's mother as a result of this relationship, but in spite of it. Men have been known to fuck anything that's physically possible—animals, slabs of liver, inflatable dolls, their own children, dead bodies, each other, so it's mere drama to single out mothers for psychological treatment. Labels are pointless when you get down to it."

Shortly after this, a fight breaks out on the other side of the room. Reuben leans over from the next table and says, "The mating ritual in this place is head-butts from ten feet."

Around one o'clock the music stops, lights are brightened, and staff wander around ordering everyone to drink up. As the bar is clearing, Rosa begins shoving chairs aside and shouting that someone has stolen her purse. Art and I stay behind to help her look for it, but get out of the way when she starts turning over tables. Bouncers come running. They are surprisingly conciliato-ry, and tell her to phone the next day in case someone turns it in. The two of us then manage to steer her through the door, down the stairs, and out onto the sidewalk.

There's a snap to the autumn night air. A lot of people are milling about out front. While Rosa is still raving about her purse, a large blonde turns to her and snarls, "Are you talking to me, honey? Are you saying *I* stole your purse?"

Her heavy black friend steps forward. "Maybe she thinks *I* took it."

"Fuck off," Rosa says.

The first woman tears off her jacket. Her big arms are tattooed. The second one throws down her purse. I get between them and say, "Listen, if you're going to fight, at least make it one on one."

Rosa seems to reassess the situation, and tells them, "Look, I'm not saying you stole it. Somebody fucking stole it but I don't know who." That appears to mollify them, and they drift away. I glance at Art who's leaning against the wall with his hands in his pockets, and walk over to the curb to look for a streetcar.

Suddenly there's a commotion behind me. I push through the crowd to see Rosa and the black woman rolling across the pave-ment, whaling on each other. Her face seems to be covered in blood, but it's a blur. I can barely follow the action, and can't fig-ure out where our girl has found all this energy on alcohol and tranquilizers. It's obvious that she's getting the worst of it, though, so I step into the eye of the hurricane and say with what I hope is a worldly, off-handed diplomacy, "Well, let's give it another minute and then break it up."

After that, the lights go out.

I don't know how much time goes by. Everything slowly starts to come into focus as a policeman is helping me to my feet. He stares into my face and says to someone, "Yeah, it's broken. Better send him to the hospital."

Most of the people are gone, and I dazedly note that the front of my white shirt is soaked with blood as I get into the back of an ambulance van. I'm not feeling any pain though, and talk away to the attendants as we drive to East General.

Other bar casualties from the area are awaiting x-rays in the emergency ward, and still rolling in. Checking the washroom mirror, I see my swollen nose, fat lips, blackening eyes, and feel the bump on the side of my skull beneath the blood-matted hair. The ring and knuckle scrapes on my left cheek suggest that I was decked from beyond my field of vision and knocked unconscious when I hit the sidewalk, then had my face worked on.

When I ask two cops why they're sitting with a guy waiting to have his broken thumb fixed, one of them answers that he stabbed someone who's in surgery upstairs. After that, people end up sharing their stories. When I tell mine, I add, "Since I have no idea who hit me, I'm afraid to go back to the O.P. in case some little old lady hobbles up to me on her cane and asks, 'Hey, didn't I kick the shit out of you?'"

"You were stupid for trying to help," the cop declares. "Chivalry's dead."

After they leave, I pass out the rest of the Valiums. Hours go by. The doctor finally bundles me in lead and has me lie on the table for x-rays. There is no skull fracture, but he says one more punch would have broken my nose. I am given a sheet listing my condition as, "Assaulted face and poss. head inj.," then booked to return as an outpatient. It's about five in the morning.

Rosa had no idea what happened to me. I later learn that she lost the fight but tried to keep it going while the woman was walking away, and went to the hospital the next day for stitches over her eye. Art tells me that a friend from his day job kicked off the guy who was straddling and punching me, and says that the police had been watching everything from their cruiser before they decided to stroll across the street and clear the sidewalk. When I ask what he was doing during all this, he hesitates. "You were out cold the whole time, right?"

"Yeah."

"I was right in there fighting. Man, my knuckles are *still* sore."

15

On a cold weekend at the far end of our back yard beyond the hedge near the sooty patch of dirt where autumn leaves were burned, my father, in a sporting mood, ran up to kick my yellow soccer ball, and it exploded with a bang, leaving a ripped piece of material by the cherry grove where I once dug for dinosaur bones.

My grade three teacher held a penmanship contest, which I won through great perseverance and was awarded a 69-cent book where you cut out the pages and folded them together to make replicas of old automobiles. I didn't bother with this, and just saved it for the inscription which said, "To Lane: the best writer in the class."

I was elected secretary of a new club because of the penmanship prize, but my talent was never put to use. We just met at a different house every Saturday and played road hockey, ate lunch and watched TV. It folded the week before it was to take place at my home.

Although my elderly grade four teacher was scary, she was fond of tricks to help us remember the spelling of words. A principle factor and the principal of a school, for example—the principal is your "pal." The surprise in surprise is that there's no "z" in "prise." She claimed that people returned ten or fifteen years later to tell her that they still remembered these associations. I know I do. I feel an obligation.

Yes, she had a reputation for being a bitch, and had me stand one day while she bawled me out for daydreaming. I should always be on my toes, she told me. If I was in a car and I was going to hit somebody, I had to make a decision to put on the brakes or

steer in the other direction; there was no automatic ejector seat. I
admit that she had a point. Looking back, it seems as if half the
time my head was in the clouds. When I was sick my parents let
me keep the kitchen radio on my bed. I played it quietly after I
should have been asleep, moving the needle across the illuminated dial in the darkness and sometimes picking up distant U.S.
cities, which thrilled me. I loved America and would send away
for tourist brochures describing such states as Maryland and
North Dakota.

My father explained that homosexuals were afraid of women,
that you couldn't trust people with very pale blue eyes, and that
our gender was superior, gently hushing my protests—even on
traditional female turf like cooking, the famous world chefs were
male, the voices of choirboys sounded more angelic than girls, etc.
He also pointed out that while an intoxicated fellow was disgust-
ing, there was nothing worse than a drunken woman.

Paradoxes existed in the determinedly masculine, however,
for he didn't believe in hunting and sarcastically dismissed the
teenager next door who shot a bird, by saying it made him feel
like a *man*. The same reason, he explained, that another neighbour
had eight children. I later wondered about that since it only
proved that Mr. X had sex with his wife eight times. His machis-
mo might have been something special if he'd had that number
of offspring with different women.

My father said my bad attitude was causing my mother
anguish, and threatened to send me to a child psychiatrist. He
took me to a film about Oliver Twist and sniffed loudly during
the boy's sad songs and tender plea for more gruel.

I could have shot the old man so often it makes my head spin
to think about it. I constantly fantasized about it. When I was nine
or ten I didn't want to wear a helmet to ride on the back of his
motorcycle because people teased me, so he clouted me around
my bedroom in a rage, and even kicked me a few good ones on
the floor, demanding, "Are you going to be a *sissy*?"

"Yes! *Yes!*" I shouted defiantly, suffering his foot at my
hindquarters which I suspected was aimed at the back of my little scrotum, emphasizing the contempt in which he held me.

The best one I ever got off at my father, circa 1966:

We were driving somewhere when he recounted how he once punched a homosexual who propositioned him, and I idly remarked, "Funny, I can't imagine you hitting anyone but me."

"Well, *thank* you," he answered, stung, unable to take his hand from the wheel to belt me.

My mother was such a WASP that she only expressed her caustic revelations to me, being a kindred spirit of sorts. She said that alcohol made flowers sprout from her liver. She was sensitive though emotionally reserved, and never retaliated with the fury to which stereotyping attributes other more flamboyant races. Whenever I annoyed her she distanced herself. She was also a person with whom I shared many a tearful adolescent agony, which in retrospect somewhat shames me since I don't think she's that wild about me either. I don't fault her for it, really.

But as a family we heard classical concerts, took Sunday drives after church, went skating and tobogganing. I had my spiritual faculties sharpened at Christian camp, I was enrolled in the YMCA, art, drama and baseball clubs, and had piano lessons. My father took me to see the first two Beatles movies but smashed one of my Rolling Stones albums because I was playing it too loudly on my Mickey Mouse-sized record player.

Though we get along now for the most part, I frequently dream that we're carrying on in the spirit of my childhood with him pounding up the stairs after me, yanking me out from behind the clothes in my closet and knocking me around the room. Certain nightmares are period pieces reconstructing or building upon actual conflicts, while others depict scenes of non-stop psychological or physical violence which exaggerate the reality or focus on the overriding impression of those years.

He's mellowed, and will joke around with me over a drink or two to mitigate the resentments we've fostered since my childhood. Then I might show him something I've written which he dismisses with the crack that I'm no Shakespeare, and produces a clipping from the classifieds requesting applicants for positions in Woolworth's management, adding that I'm not to drink any more of his beers because he's saving them for company.

So I avoid the fucking suburbs for another month or two.

My parents know by now that I have drifted into a horrifying mediocrity, which is of course the worst fate of all: to be plodding through a dismal existence with my ambitions unfulfilled, and my brain dissolved to trash in one ball and chain limbo after another.

16

Verna's period is late, so I take her to a pro-life agency in a converted bungalow in the east end that performs free pregnancy tests. An elderly lady confirms my fears later that day when she shows us the jar of urine and tells us that the results are positive. She offers to make an appointment for counselling, but I thank her and say that we're just going to think things over for now. Polite but determined, she follows us to the door, reciting their hours.

Gusts of wind whip around us as we walk south, not saying much. Sun occasionally breaks through the clouds. We go into a restaurant close to the subway and sit down in a booth by the window. I order a couple of coffees, trying to figure out how to begin. There doesn't seem to be any way around it. "You know," I say, "an abortion—"

Verna is expecting this of course, and interrupts me, saying, "This baby is a part of me. I can *feel* it."

"We've just known each other for a little while, whereas having a kid is a lifetime responsibility."

"I want us to have it."

"You know you're not in any position to look after a baby, and you're not taking into consideration the mixed racial angle if you were to give it up. Nobody would want to adopt it, and you know what it's like to grow up in institutions. You don't want to inflict that kind of existence on anyone just to satisfy this maternal whim of yours, do you?"

Her eyes narrow. "So you want to kill it. Aren't you kind. Well, it won't come to that because I'm going to keep it. If you don't want to stick around, then don't."

"All right," I say, "I *will* leave. Don't get the idea you can collect a family this way."

The waitress sets down the cups and saucers.

Verna tears open a packet and adds sugar. She then pours in cream and stirs her coffee in silence, smoldering. We sit in the dull light, me looking out the window, until she says, "You're a real prick, you know that?"

I put my hand on her wrist, but she pulls away. "It'll be for the best, you'll see."

"And you're still splitting anyway, right?"

"Only for a while, but like I said, maybe we can live together when I get back if you're interested."

I just need time alone to reevaluate the situation.

Verna starts having bloody discharges. Not knowing if she's suffering a miscarriage or infection, I may not be as attentive sexually. She lies naked on the bed and parts her lips with her fingers, snarling, "How come you aren't eating me? Lick me down there—lick my *cunt!*"

Our emotions flare constantly. She stalks the room like a leopard with luminous eyes and taut muscles. The two of us are balanced on the edge of a knife, but I avoid fighting with her because I don't want to break up before the abortion.

Around this time a black woman named Tibbi moves into the room next to Verna's. She wears her hair natural and likes African-style garments. By way of introduction she comes over and tells us, with her hands on her hips, that she's been fucking two guys for the past three hours, and man, is she *beat*.

We become friends in a fragmented triangle as my relationship with Verna disintegrates. They have an ambivalent alliance, as Tibbi repeats everything that my girlfriend confides to her, such as the fact that she hates me and can't wait until I leave the city.

Every day, it seems, I am more distraught by drama or tragedy. A couple with Downs Syndrome are sitting at the front of the bus, French kissing with their eyes closed, feet swinging. The young man gets off at the intersection and waves from the corner while

we pull away. His girlfriend has forgotten him however, and studies the ceiling. I look back to see him still waving with the sun in
his eyes.

An odd sensation when you run into someone about whom
you've dreamt recently, and find their image altered through no
fault of their own.

I suppose everyone's half-consciously imagined swinging
their car into the oncoming lane of traffic or suddenly leaping
before a subway train. But have you ever felt the impulse to bite
the neck off a beer bottle and crunch it with shards of glass piercing your gums, cheeks and tongue?

I suspect that cockroaches are defiling my toothbrush when
black specks reappear on the bristles. There are two outlets in the
hotel room for which I have to choose combinations of radio,
lamps, and the old black and white TV one of the East Indian
cleaners gave me that someone left behind. There's no point buying an electrical cheater since the usual conjunctions are already
sufficient to blow my power. At least I don't have to use the fan
anymore. After complaining at the desk, I discover where the
breaker panel is located and start throwing the switch myself to
restore order.

I am tiring of the web which traverses my space. Tiny
clumps of dust near the light resemble sunlit snow. I jump up to
pull it down, but the thread snaps me in the forehead before I
hit the ground. When I look closer I realize it's *dental floss*. Who
can fathom the humanity which has lived if not died in this
room before me?

I hear from Egbert Hahn that Izzy Silver went over to Tia Maria's
townhouse and mainlined coke in the bathroom, then sat around
downstairs with a few people before returning to the can. When
they heard a crash, someone went up and broke in to find him
having convulsions on the floor. The guy helped him to his feet
and tried to lean him against the door, but Izzy pulled away and
staggered out into the hall, falling down the staircase to the living
room. While barely conscious, he apparently claimed that he'd hit
seven or eight grams and swallowed another half ounce with

water. The quantity seems questionable, since I'd been of the understanding that ten grams could be taken over the course of a day, but that less than two would be a single lethal dosage. I suppose it might come down to a matter of purity. In any case, Izzy was in very bad condition and had been bleeding from the mouth when he was driven to the hospital, as the cocaine had eaten through his stomach lining. He was pronounced D.O.A.

He reportedly left behind a suicide note stating that he was unhappy over his bad luck with women and lack of true friends. If I had taken the time to properly document his weird and rowdy behaviour over the years, his death might seem as much a contradiction to the reader as to myself. His actions were often confounding and warranted a kick in the ass. This, however, appears to confirm another dimension which had surfaced recently, so of course it's rather sad.

Although I try to make the funeral with a few people, we get lost due to poor directions and arrive too late. It seems there was only a small turnout, as it was rumoured that people were worried that the police would be observing the service, or some such shit, but then I suppose Izzy showed the same indifference when DeLurgio went to pieces.

The Warwick Hotel is slated to be levelled for a parking lot, and will be through soon as well. When I go with Verna on her last night before the closure, I'm surprised to see all the publicity that has been generated. Cops are hanging around the lobby, a TV crew is shooting on the street, bikers are drinking at the next table, and there's actually a line of people clamouring to get inside. About ten hookers are partying near Verna and me between her sets, yelling endearments at Brandy with his fat gut and whirling dress. He's singing his raunchy best and cracking lines like, "There's bullshit and there's con men . . . Hey, you fuckers—why don't I meet you at the bar for a quickie? Play a church on fire and I'll piss all over you!"

A newspaper article about the closing says that our drag queen is fifty-four years old and performed in carnival side shows, gay bars and strip joints for thirty years before finally establishing a home at the Warwick, a place he seemed to personify with his rude Irish humour. Brandy lived in a room down the corridor from the manager's office, and claimed to have had four wives, nine husbands, and half a dozen children. He's moving on to another lounge in a small city to the east, but as far as I'm concerned, he should be struck by lightning on this last night while belting out his final "Hello, Dolly."

The hotel was constructed in 1910 and was known as the Royal Cecil, a respectable locale in a classy district prior to the area's decline. It became the Warwick in 1948. I remember the first night I was ever here, back in the early '70s. I was sitting with a friend across the aisle from two couples, when one of the men and his girlfriend got into an argument, and stood up and started smacking each other. A waiter ran over and pacified them, and they took their seats. When the same thing happened again, it was clearly her fault and she was ushered out of the bar, but five minutes later came back and took to walloping him a third time. As the waiter put down his full tray to grab her, she succeeded in flipping it in a crash of beer and glasses over her boyfriend.

Another incident which wasn't so amusing occurred when a patron had a disagreement with a waiter, and stood up to throw a bad punch. Six evil waiters in red jackets suddenly flew over from all ends of the bar, beating him to the floor and putting their boots to him. After that, he was thrown out.

This last night of the Warwick is a better occasion, however, as prostitutes break empty glasses and the bikers howl. A few other dancers come by and hug Verna. Seriously, Brandy should die from a shattered bottle and be frozen for time immemorial at his peak.

There's still a line-up to get in when I leave briefly for some pizza. This joker with a shaved head from a rock and roll station approaches me with a gigantic tape recorder strapped over his shoulder, and asks if I lost my innocence in there. "No," I answer into the microphone, "but I did lose fifty dollars on a hooker, which was the lousiest fifty dollars I ever spent." When people in the background laugh, I elaborate by telling him how the girls turned their tricks up at Larry's Hideaway.

17

I quit my job and get ready to head west. Before I can leave, however, Verna and I take a Greyhound to Buffalo, NY for what should be a straightforward abortion to bypass the local red tape. Perhaps she hasn't travelled very much and is enthused by the sense of adventure or camaraderie, I'm not sure, but she's in very good spirits and we seem to be friends again for the first time in weeks. I hold her hand while we look out the window. Although it's fairly cold, the sun is bright and the scenery along the QEW offers a break from the city.

From the bus depot in the U.S.A. we take a taxi to the hospital. The black cabby isn't particularly friendly. When we get out and walk into the building, I ask her, "Did you find he had some kind of attitude? About my being with you, maybe?"

She laughs. "Yeah, sure, but everyone turning to stare at us in the station was even crazier. It was like a row of cards falling down, you know?"

At the information desk we're directed to the right floor. I've never liked the antiseptic odour or well-lit desperation of hospitals, and maybe to lighten the mood I tell her, "Listen, if you did have a miscarriage and aren't pregnant anymore, I'll buy you a dress with the money instead."

The receptionist gives me a tourist map and suggests that I come back in a couple of hours, so I leave. While wandering the streets early that afternoon, I wonder what to do about the relationship. It appears be on the upswing, but that could change again, of course.

Although I've presented myself in a less than sympathetic light with her, there is no denying that she and I have an important bond. Maybe not enough to change my mind about leaving for now, since I've committed myself to the idea, but it seems possible that we might still somehow keep it together.

Later, when I return to the hospital, Verna rushes over to me in the lobby looking excited and happy. "I *miscarried*," she says.

"What, really?"

"When I told them everything that had been happening with the discharging and everything, they did a fast urine test and said I wasn't pregnant."

"And that's it?"

She fixes the collar of my jacket. "Well, they said it would be a good idea to have another test in Toronto after we go home just to make sure." With an uncertain smile she says, "So… don't forget your promise. You said you were going to buy me a dress."

"You're right, I did."

We have a late lunch, then do some shopping. She picks up a cute denim outfit in a downtown boutique. After that we take the bus to one of the sights on my map, the Albright-Knox art museum, and I snap a couple of photos of her on the lawn by a red abstract sculpture, posing as if she's on the cover of *Vogue*. In the background there's a statue of a horse and rider in front of a row of columns. I remember that she'd once said she'd wanted to be a model. Yes, it is adventure.

Back at the station later that afternoon, we decide to stop at the coffee shop before our departure. While we're sitting in a booth, I notice a big black mother in an army jacket and beret checking us out from the doorway. He saunters over. Sliding in next to my woman, he puts his sunglasses by the salt shaker, and says, "What's happening?"

"Not much." Ignoring him, I ask Verna what she's having.

She looks uneasy. "I don't know. I'm not that hungry."

"Dig this," the hustler says. "I got a little coke if you're interested. We can slide around the corner to my place, and I'll lay a snort on my man and his lady."

I almost consider it, but tell him, "We don't have any money, so it wouldn't be worth your while. Thanks anyway."

He gets up reluctantly and puts on his shades. "Yeah . . . Well, stay cool."

As he's walking away, Verna looks at me. "I almost thought you were going to say yes."

"Yeah, that would have been stupid."

When it's time to catch the bus, we pay our bill at the register. Outside, the same dealer is leaning against the wall with three other brothers who catcall Verna about her fine ass, etc. Of course I have to wonder if the coke was just a front to get us to his place in order to fuck us up. The races continue to harbour natural suspicions of one another and resent outsiders messing with their women. Although I don't suffer from white guilt, I don't really blame those studs or the cab driver or the blacks in the bus station. Word on the street is, Whitey has fucked them over and should stay the hell away.

On the ride home it's difficult to see the landscape beyond reflections in the window. I look at my shadowed image, then move closer to the glass and cup my hand around my eye to observe the countryside in twilight. Crossing the bridge near Hamilton, the white lights, smokestacks and steel plant fires are reflected in the dark, polluted water.

I've probably been unfair by emphasizing Verna's bad qualities. As I was trying to say, we've spent significant time together, and I guess I'm appreciating the relationship more at the moment. It's intense, this impression that I'm both loved and hated.

I kiss her forehead and fondle her breasts, slipping my hand under the fabric to squeeze and pull each stiffening nipple. She touches my crotch, examining the high relief of denim. The seats around us near the back are vacant, and the lighting is dim. I unzip and ease my jeans down my hips, and we smile at one another as she holds my cock. Sexually, anyway, we're magic together.

"Why don't you go down on me?" I say. "It'll be a good episode for your diary."

"How can I here?"

"We'll cover you with the jackets so it'll look like you're asleep if anyone comes by."

Verna manages to lie across the seats. I hold one armrest and caress the back of her neck as she sucks me. Each jolt is conveyed through her teeth, however. Wincing as she nips me again, I say, "Um . . . listen, thanks, but I think this ride's too rocky."

She sits up looking a little sulky until I guide her fingers.

Taking her Kleenex from her purse, she begins to jack me off beneath the jackets. For some reason a black man is suddenly standing in the aisle in front of us, and she pulls away.

"'Scuse me," he says. "You got a light?"

I sigh as she looks for some matches.

He strikes one under his cigarette. Exhaling, he hands them back with a wink, and says, "One more time."

We glance at each other. She laughs as he walks away, but I don't want to lose my state of grace, and redirect her hand.

A couple of days later, Verna and I have an appointment at that East York clinic for a confirmation pregnancy test. I've booked the midnight train to Edmonton, checked out of the Isabella, and put my stuff at her place. We're scheduled to get the results late that afternoon, but the atmosphere in her room grows increasingly ugly again as she prowls for a fight, ready to spit whenever she looks at me. The situation has become quite torturous, really, and it seems clear that whatever affection she was showing me during our trip was phony or at the very least superficial, and it's time to just get the hell out of town.

Barefoot, I step on a fucking tack, right into the heel. She's not particularly sympathetic as I limp to the washroom to bring back some disinfectant. While I'm swabbing the puncture, Verna looks up from her magazine and sneers, "Don't get your blood on anything."

"Shut up," I answer, and toss the Q-Tip at her.

Well, she picks up a glass ashtray and hurls it at me. It hits the wall by my head, then she's across the room in a flash, punching me. I smack her a couple of times and push her down on the bed, hard.

"Get out!" she yells.

I go over to the library for an hour or two.

When I come back, she's watching TV.

"Are you ready to go to the clinic?" I ask, standing in the doorway.

She doesn't look up. "No."

"When *will* you be ready?"

"Tomorrow."

"You know I'm leaving tonight. We have to go now."

"I don't care if you're there or not."

Leaning against the jamb, I say, "We have to make sure you're out of trouble before I go, and they won't tell me anything unless you're there too. What was that number they assigned you?"

"None of your business."

"All right, fine. Good luck."

I collect my knapsack and leave.

At the subway station I sit on a bench by the turnstiles, wondering what to do as the rush hour throng passes me. Finally, I decide to try the clinic myself, and go down the stairs to the southbound track.

At Bloor/Danforth I head east to Coxwell, and take the escalator up to the street level. I could catch a bus, but I'm restless and prefer to walk. It's a working to middle class neighbourhood with modest, well-tended properties. The trees by now have lost most of their leaves, and it feels like we're on the edge of winter.

When I get there and knock on the door, a gray-haired woman opens up. "Excuse me," I say, "I know you've got a policy on giving out information, but this is an emergency."

She steps back and holds it open. "Come in."

A stout woman about sixty joins us in the hallway. When I explain that my girlfriend and I have broken up, that I'm leaving the city and want to make sure everything's okay, she commends what she calls my sense of responsibility.

We walk down the hall to the back room where the samples are stored, and look for Verna's jar. The older woman finds it, and holds it up to the light. Peering through her glasses, she says, "The results are positive."

I don't believe it. "She's *pregnant*?"

The other one confirms it. "Oh, yes, this is a very reliable test."

I leave in a kind of daze, and walk back to the subway. It's cold, and getting dark.

In the station I try to analyze the situation. I don't want to see Verna anymore, I can no longer handle the hospital costs, I have a ticket out of here. But I have to go back. Although I don't really like the women who live next door to her, I decide that maybe I should talk to them. Hoisting my gear, I pay another token and get on the westbound train.

Half an hour later I'm crossing the park to Summerhill Gardens, having almost figured out what to say. I probably come across as a bit off my head when I gather them in their second floor kitchen and tell them that if they're really her friends they'll help her now. Going over the situation, I offer to give them a hundred and twenty-five dollars towards the abortion if they could possibly kick in with me and maybe see her through it. They accept the money a little bewilderedly, and say okay.

As I'm going down the stairs towards their front door, Verna comes in with an expectant expression. "Are you looking for me?" I guess she saw me heading to the house next door through her window.

I'm too harassed at this point to be polite. "Yes," I say, walking past her. "You're still knocked up."

"I'm *pregnant*?" She follows me outside and grabs my arm.

"Don't worry. I gave them some money, and they're going to help you."

Suddenly she's angry again. "What? Don't you think I've got any pride?"

"I don't care one way or another," I say, freeing myself. "So long."

Verna grabs me again. "Don't go! I'm afraid of the abortion. Stay until it's over."

"Look, there's no point. We don't get along."

"Please! I won't be a bitch anymore, I promise."

Well, I'm at a crossroads. I'd have to stay overnight which would mean more fighting. And then there's the matter of my ticket. After a minute, I tell her that I'll find out if I can delay my train ride another day and try to fix things, but I can't make any promises. I'm uneasy as she slips her arm through mine and walks me towards her place.

Unexpectedly, the railroad company does allow me to alter my departure time by another twenty-four hours, so I unpack my toothbrush.

In the morning I conduct further research and miraculously discover that a hospital here in the city has an inexpensive abortion set-up that isn't even contingent upon Verna having a health card, which she doesn't. I collect my money from the women next door, take her down for a check-up, schedule an appointment, and give her enough cash to help keep her expenses covered.

Of course, that evening we're enemies again. My wild black girl with her high-boned face and flashing eyes, husky voice and hair-trigger temper, does her predatory stalk while the TV plays and her cat lazes in a chair. Naturally we have an argument and she storms from the room.

As I'm preparing to leave, Verna returns and puts her arms around me, her eyes brimming. Then she bursts out crying. "I can't live without you! Don't you *know* that?"

"Look, I thought you hated me."

"I tried to believe I didn't need you anymore because you were leaving and wouldn't take me with you."

She's really bawling, unlike anything I've seen. I'm on a roller coaster with these emotional upheavals, and feel my sympathies swing again. Giving her a hug, I tell her that she shouldn't look at it that way. I'll miss her. She swears she'll be faithful and just wait for me to come home, which, despite her apparent sincerity, seems pretty unlikely, so I smile as I dry her eyes and ask her to keep me in mind; if she's not married, we'll get back together. I just have to go away and save up some money for a few months, that's all.

18

I used to look up to a kid across the street named Sal, who was a year older than I and won every fight I'd seen him in, including one on my behalf when somebody took my bike. He had a gruff voice and smoked from an early age. Sal was also our street's best hockey and baseball player, and pitched in a local club where I played second base. I was comparatively lousy, and so uninvolved that I thought nothing of breaking my own team trophy during a tantrum. When I finally came up against him in a club game, I was surprised when he slowly lobbed the ball to me as if I was five years old. Since I got a good hit off it and he'd risked the ire of his team who had no idea that we knew one another, I decided that his seeming condescension was ultimately a friendly gesture. He could have easily fired that ball across the plate and fucked me right up. I later managed to grow my hair longer than him and smoked dope first, which seemed to impress him, but he was the popular one with girls, played guitar, and dropped acid before me.

When I was about ten I was sitting at the kitchen table eating lunch after church, when my mother saw him pull an apple off our tree. She was standing by the sink, and called out the window, "Sal! Do you know what that's called?"

My soup spoon froze.

"An apple?"

"No, it's called *stealing*!"

I laughed and could see that she couldn't help being amused herself. There was nothing of the charmer in younger Bobby, however, who she considered a shifty, disrespectful scamp. When she once upbraided him about something, he just turned and spat on the sidewalk. I was impressed by how brazenly he'd steal money and smokes from his mother's purse.

Although Bobby was two years Sal's junior, there was a period when the three of us hung out together. Sal liked the fact that he had no qualms about shoplifting, and would do anything he told him to. On one occasion I was biting into the stolen ice cream sandwich Bobby was still holding, when the owner ran out of the store and grabbed him. As he hauled him back inside to call his parents, Sal said to me, "Hey, when we came out of my house and I saw a mail truck go by, I made a wish on it that he'd get caught today."

I was shocked but figured that if one could even make a successful wish on a mail truck, it had to have been spontaneous, because he certainly had no ill will towards Bobby.

Sal was grounded one day and wasn't allowed to have anybody in, but when his parents went out he invited Bobby up to his room. Unfortunately, they came home while he was still there, so Sal made the kid jump out his second floor window in his stocking feet. He got into trouble anyway, because Bobby's shoes were still down by the front door.

At Christian summer camp in 1966, I asked my counsellor that if Heaven was ecstasy, would I be forced to listen to the classical music associated with angels, or would I be permitted to hear rock and roll? He paused and then told me that such musicians were for the most part atheists and would thus be excluded from Heaven as would their music.

We may go to church throughout our young lives, the leaders informed us, and yet may never make a personal commitment to God. Christianity wasn't something with which we were blessed eternally at baptism but rather a conscious step we ourselves had to take at our moment of awareness. This wasn't unlike Kierkegaard's religious philosophy as I remember it, responsibility being the essence of existentialism.

As the lights went out one night, I made a shy prayer requesting entry into the holy domain and inscribed within my heart the principles of Jesus, then turned over and whispered to my counsellor in the next bed that I was a Christian now. He propped himself on his elbow and asked when this happened, apparently surprised that an act of such magnitude could be so brief. I nonetheless shivered with joy, being an individual who existed in God's sphere in the company of such icons as Noah and Moses.

On the homebound bus I was reading from my stack of comic books when an older boy asked to look at one. I explained that I didn't want to lend them out because I'd never get them all back, but was shamed into it when he pointed out that I obviously hadn't learned anything at camp. They were passed around and later returned intact, proving my selfish fears unfounded.

Back home, I sat with my mother on the sofa and tried to tell her of my religious experience, but found myself crying for no good reason while she attempted to understand.

A rare compliment from my father made an impression when he said something to the effect that my sensitivity indicated high intelligence. While I was sullenly helping him work on the dock at the cottage, however, he told me that I was as useless as tits on a bull.

I won a competition designing a logo for the North York Youth Safety Council, which got printed on their stationary. I also won an *Uncle Bobby* colouring contest in the newspaper, but went to the annual Sunday school picnic instead of a movie with the other prizewinners.

That winter, in grade six, there was a small gathering after school where kids were going to play spin the bottle. I walked over with a new boy named Joe, a Native Indian who was considered hip for his long hair and pointed boots. When we got there, the host told us that his mother said it was too crowded, so only Joe could come in. As Joe turned to leave with me, Leonard tried to call him back, but he spit into a snow bank and said, "If you don't want my friend, you don't want me either." I don't think I've ever experienced such loyalty, and still feel grateful.

Leonard later phoned my house to tell us that his mother relented and that we could both come over. I discussed it with Joe before accepting. Maybe I had sufficient backbone to refuse but felt a responsibility to my friend and wanted to prove myself to whatever girl may have objected to my playing.

After school on a mild fall afternoon in grade seven, Anthony, Mark and I stood talking outside my home. I transferred my books to my other arm and slowly held out my hand in front of Anthony, finger and thumb forming a circle. When he accidentally glanced down, I punched him on the shoulder. (If someone was aware of anybody making this gesture without actually looking at it and managed to insert a finger into the circle before it could be pulled away, he punched his adversary three times. If he unthinkingly turned to the hand, he was punched once.)

"You asshole," Anthony laughed.

"Ah, Delvecchio," Mark laughed. "You *goof*."

I saw a young deaf woman whom I recognized from the neighbourhood approaching. Although we were strangers, I was a smart-ass and stepped out to present her with the sign, then tried to explain the game by repeatedly poking the circle with the index finger of my other hand. Her face registered horror.

What happened next seemed to occur in slow motion: I closed my eyes as she took a step backwards, swinging her arm, and caught a walloping slap that almost turned my head around. I laughed with Anthony and Mark as she hurried away, a little puzzled by the severity of her reaction. We either overlooked or didn't recognize my inadvertent obscenity, unless I've subconsciously reworked the details.

There was a newspaper story about Mark a couple of years later that I saved:

FUGITIVE NABBED UNDER BED

A 14-year-old escapee from a training school who has outdistanced police in an estimated fifty cat chases since Halloween, was caught yesterday under a bed. Plainclothed officers saw the boy yesterday driving a flashy new car. They recognized his trademark—a floppy sombrero-type hat and blond wig. The boy spotted the officers and he took off. Three hours later, police were called to investigate the theft of watches and wallets from N—— Secondary School in North York. Police learned the identity of one suspect. They went to his house to arrest him. Then they found the long-sought boy under a bed. He faces 17 charges including housebreaking, car theft and failing to remain at the scene of an accident.

To stimulate interest in the upcoming federal election, our grade seven history teacher asked us to state our political parties of choice and choose leaders among ourselves to run for mock office. Too ignorant to have such opinions ourselves, we imitated our parents. When I stood up with the Progressive Conservatives, the others elected me head of the party and it became my responsibility to write and deliver a few speeches, shake some hands, etc. After the campaign was over, votes were to be cast independent of anyone's outside affiliations.

Following the views presented by the NDP leader and myself, the Liberal candidate told the teacher he thought his speech writer was going to prepare something for him, and had to stand in front of everyone for three or four minutes anyway, looking stupid.

After a couple of weeks on the hustings I won the election and became Prime Minister of Canada.

I'd been at odds with my parents over the length of my hair since I was nine, getting square-back cuts at the barber and spending ages combing my hair into ducktails and pompadours, but it got serious in the second half of the sixties when rock culture went psychedelic and *Life* magazine was covering Haight-Ashbury. Although I finally arrived at an understanding with my mother at thirteen, my father told me one day that that I better have it cut off by the time he got home from work. He didn't take my threats to run away seriously, so I collected my cash, bank book and birth certificate, and went to junior high intending to withdraw my money afterwards on the way to the bus station. In a twist of fate about 10:15, I was called to the office to find him waiting in the hall. Much to my surprise he said that my mother persuaded him to change his mind. As I dug into my pockets to return his barber money, I pulled out the aforementioned items, which may have indicated that my plans for travelling were real.

Years later his fears were no doubt realized when I ran with a stoned and disreputable crowd. One evening as my best friend

Ian and another guy were waiting out front in a VW with a bad
muffler, he shouted out the door after me, "Remember what I
told you!"

They turned around. "So, what did he tell you?"

"Not to do anything illegal."

Ian was a speed freak who kindly hit me up with crystal meth
for the first time when I was sixteen, and later introduced me to
Sean Cochrane. We rode on his motorcycle, chased girls, drove to
Montreal… After he dropped out of school he set an example of
self-indulgence that I still find impressive in retrospect; when I
would knock on his door I'd witness his ritual of smoking dope
as soon as he rolled out of bed in the mornings. Later on, as is
often the case with best pals, we fell out over one thing or another and ended up enemies. He bested me in our first fight, I won
the second, and the third was about even when it got broken up.

After high school I enrolled in a journalism program before
ending up in university. One night on what was supposed to be
MDA, Ian and I were slumming at our favourite dive where the
bouncer had once thrown a customer into our table and picked
his knife up from the floor, and found ourselves sitting near an old
derelict who kept mumbling to himself that he used to be a big
jewel thief. I didn't have much of a taste for alcohol that night and
assumed he needed it more, so I pushed my beers across the table
to him.

Afterwards, as we were wandering north, we passed a roadway to the old Toronto Jail and thought it might be interesting to
explore. The building not only seemed ominous and gothic, but
under the influence of the hallucinogenic we thought we could
hear yelling from inside. There had, after all, been allegations of
prisoner abuse in the papers. For kicks I shouted, "I am a journal-
ist and I am your saviour, and I will spread news of your oppres-
sion to the world!" Ian was further alarmed when I climbed the
fence, and swore from below that he was going to leave if I did-
n't come down.

A guard came out looking heavy, and demanded to know
what we were doing. I said that as concerned taxpayers we were
giving the jail an inspection. Ian had a gaunt face and long frizzy

hair that stuck out in all directions, so he probably looked even more suspicious than I did. Although he'd been in a bit of a panic when I was messing around, he got into the spirit at that point with some improvisation of his own. Another guard then appeared and asked what we were up to. "I don't know," his colleague answered, "but they might not think it's so fucking funny if we put them in jail for the night."

After that, as we were sitting in the Don Valley watching the pretty lights of passing traffic, Ian turned to me looking wasted, and said in a tone reminiscent of Dorothy telling Toto that she didn't believe they were in Kansas anymore, "Lane, you know, I think we're on *acid*."

On an unrelated note, I had been drinking in a very noisy bar over a period of hours one evening and was trying to make a phone call to a guy named Eddie Archibald. I couldn't hear very well, and for some reason kept getting the wrong bloody number. The next morning at the breakfast table my father said, "Last night this strange person kept calling here, asking for somebody named 'Archibald'."

19

I observe the dark industrial landscape near the railway tracks as the train leaves the city. Over the next three days it rolls northwest through the increasingly rugged terrain of Ontario, skirting Lake Superior and crossing Manitoba. In the stark prairies I take some PCP with some people in the bar car before we depart Saskatchewan for the province of Alberta, north of cowboy country.

In Edmonton I check into a mission. The neighbourhood is grim but the building itself is clean and equipped with modern facilities. There are about twenty beds per room in the lower level, where the odours of wine and socks linger in a depressing bouquet. The next morning as we're standing in line for coffee, porridge and toast, some wastrel threatens to knife me when I get tired of listening to him bitch about the place and ask him what he's doing here. It's a free ride as far as I'm concerned; nobody forced him. Despite his ugly overcoat he's hardly beyond redemption. "I'll *kill* you," he sputters. "I'll *stab* you to death. I'm wanted for murder right now."

A couple of days later I hitchhike north to Fort McMurray, which is something of a boom town due to the extraction of crude oil from the tar sands. The final stretch of highway cuts through flat, barren country distinguished by muskeg and small pine trees, to a hill overlooking the last frontier: a mosaic of low-rise buildings and trailers bordered by evergreens and the Athabaska River.

I get a job in the kitchen of a camp catering to a large outfit laying sewer pipes, and wash dishes, peel potatoes, fill the milk dispensers and mop the floor. The swarthy French Canadian cook talks about working in the Arctic and the subsequent culture shock when returning to the city—how he has to lock himself in his room for a week or two with a few cases of beer. He comes on to me half-drunkenly and ends up getting fired for going on a two-day bender. His successor gets the axe when he's discovered loading supplies into a truck one night for his restaurant in Calgary.

Verna doesn't have a phone, so I call her at Tibbi's number the day of the abortion. She tells me coldly that she had a miscarriage after all. I assume that she's less than forthcoming because our conversation is being overheard, but she doesn't answer my letter either.

Tibbi, however, responds to the one I mailed her:

" . . .Verna, I regret to say, is really through with you but doesn't know how to break the news. She was courted by two guys as soon as you left, and the latest one, who just took off for Vancouver, was living with her for a week. He was called Jake and I thought he was a real pig, no fucking jive. Please do *not* mention what I said. I have to tell you because I like you and don't want you to get hurt when you return . . ."

Although I don't really blame Verna, I resent how she's handled it, and write to her unequivocally ending things. In a separate letter to Tibbi I claim that I could pick up with my ex-girlfriend where I left off if I felt like it, despite her bullshit theatrics. That's how I lay it down, anyway.

She replies: " . . . Verna's singing in a group right now, and apparently the gig is on the move. She hasn't collected her mail, so I'm sending your letter back if it's still there when I come home from work today. In the one you wrote to me you sounded like you wanted to cut her brown throat . . ." There is a P.S. that the letter in question has been removed, so I guess that's it.

I have to wonder about it all, having since learned that discharges are a normal symptom of pregnancy. I'm trying to remember if there really was blood in those secretions. Surely the doctor in Buffalo would have questioned our interpretation and proceeded with the abortion regardless, unless Verna cancelled the appointment after I planted the stupid idea of that dress. A hospital couldn't have

expected her to eject and dispose of a dead fetus on her own, even
if they thought she had miscarried. And was there even enough time
for a urine test? I hadn't been thinking straight.

And yet she did seem genuinely shocked when I told her she
was still pregnant. If there's reason to suspect she wasn't telling the
truth in Buffalo, it follows that she could have lied about the miscarriage over the phone also. Maybe I'm a father-to-be.

I become friends with a big, longhaired American drifter
who favours bib overalls, wears granny glasses, and plays bluegrass
banjo. He confides that he's only been laid once in his life—
Denver, 1974—and was at one stage too shattered to leave his
apartment each morning until first drinking a bottle of wine.

A rangy foreman with a gray crew-cut tells us that some of
the good old boys back home in North Carolina lost their cherries to Negro whores, and thereafter only had sex with such
women. When the opportunity would finally arise to make it
with white females, they couldn't manage it unless the girls pulled
on black stockings for the necessary illusion.

"You know you're a good fuck," he says, "when a hooker
gives you the second one for free." Well, how the hell are you supposed to impress them if you're not allowed to make them come?

Victor, another kitchen employee, used to work in a tire fac-
tory in Montreal. He is an odd but amusing little character in his
forties with dark curly hair and perpetual whiskers, who, with his
darting eyes, resembles a rather large rodent when he's nibbling
food in the canteen. The hitchhiker he rolled into town with confirmed my suspicions before he quit by telling me that when they
bunked together, Victor had tried to seduce him. My coworker
apparently believes his predilection is so well concealed that he
can afford to dance around the subject by joking while we're
washing dishes that my ass should be greased with butter, and
informing me, incorrectly, that Simon and Garfunkel are gay.

The man follows me into the showers after a lunch shift, and
nonchalantly watches me while soaping himself in the opposite
stall. At the sinks that evening he remarks out of the blue, "Just like
I thought—you've got a big cock. Tall, thin guys like you always
have big cocks."

"And how would you know that?"

He hesitates. "Because I'm short, and so is my dick."

I'm depressed and somewhat lonely, and try to pick up a rough-looking squaw at The Oil Sands bar in town one night, but she leaves with somebody else. Although I've never questioned my sexual orientation, I consider Victor's fawning attention and make the standard rationalization that he's not too pretty, but if I close my eyes and imagine he's a girl, I wouldn't really be compromising my masculinity.

A few days later when Victor's making the usual banter, I say, "Look, I know you're queer, so you can stop pretending you're not."

This throws him, even scares him, and he tries to look offended. "Can't a guy make a few innocent jokes without somebody saying something like that?"

"Look, whatever. Your friend told me. If you want to blow me, come over to my room after work." Then I add casually, "But you're going to have to swallow all of it."

Victor is confused, and doesn't answer. Later, however, he shows up at my door in our long aluminum trailer. He's a little inhibited in case I'm trying to set him up, and makes silly conversation as he sits beside me on the bed, flipping through a magazine. The walls of the small room have fake wood panelling.

I'm mildly intrigued by the psychological aspect of subjugating a male eager to play the passive role. I tend to feel that a woman will go down on you in a mutually lustful situation, to show her affection, or at the very least to reciprocate. It's a different, subtler chemistry. A strange piece of rough trade, on the other hand, will happily just get down on his knees for you behind a garbage can.

"I thought you wanted to suck me off," I say.

He giggles and makes a playful grab for my johnson. I lock the door, then stand in front of him and unbuckle my pants.

On December 8th I learn that John Lennon has been killed. The world is echoing with the news. After he fell onto the sidewalk with Yoko Ono screaming, the doorman apparently asked his murderer if he realized what he'd done, and this Chapman fuck-er answered that he had just shot J.L.

I reel with both the deaths of my childhood and one of my greatest heroes, and can't help crying in my room. I remember my father offering to buy me my first record when we were in a department store, and I picked the only thing I recognized, the number one song on the singles chart, "She Loves You." This was an act of generosity for which I have always given him credit. The world is falling apart with the disappearance of my luminaries, and grief is usually to some extent selfish.

The timing is tragic in that Lennon had recently expressed his distaste for the notion of burning out early, and admired sur-vivors like Gloria Swanson. It couldn't have happened at a better time to insure his immortality, however, given his return to the recording studio after years of seclusion to produce a new single ironically titled "Starting Over." John wasn't interested in the early death syndrome however, so fuck it.

History bulldozes forward. I actually feel sorrier for McCartney, having to survive such mass adulation which partial-ly eclipses his role in the phenomenon, the bad press he's received musically, and his efforts to be gracious in the face of his ex-part-ner's bastard sniping, which he endured for years.

On an earth of mortal gods the calendar should be changed. 1981 will become 1 A.D.: the first year after the departures of Lennon, Henry Miller, Jean-Paul Sartre, Alfred Hitchcock, Peter Sellers, Jimmy Durante, Katherine Anne Porter, the Warwick Hotel, Steve McQueen, bank robber Willie Sutton, Mae West, and Jesse Owens—the black athlete who won four gold medals at the 1936 Olympics and undermined Hitler's attempt to present Aryan supremacy at the Berlin Games. Plus Izzy Silver, for that matter. This of course is to ignore the millions of others around the world whose existences were extinguished for all time before the dawn of the new millennium.

20

I'm in a low frame of mind with winter closing over me. I haven't managed to land a better job, as it seems the frozen earth may have slowed down construction, and the giant tar sand projects outside town are unionized. I quit the camp and return to Edmonton.

While staying in another mission I scour newspapers and employment centres, cold-call companies, and get hired as an oil-rig roughneck. I'm told to take a bus up to a place called Slave Lake, off the southwestern point of Lesser Slave Lake. A motel will have my reservation. I get my gear and ride after nightfall through more wild country with tiny towns and hamlets, where passengers whose lives I can only imagine carry their bags down the steps and get off into darkness.

I hang around the motel and watch TV the next day. An oil truck is supposed to pick me up that night at about two in the morning to take me almost three hundred miles further north, so I try to catch a bit of shut-eye in the evening with no luck. When the rig pulls into the parking lot, I toss my knapsack into the cab as I climb in, and say hello to a bearded driver who's grinning at me with one eye off centre and a cowboy hat on his head. He takes the cigar out of his mouth as we shake hands, and tells me his name is Nick.

When he finally stops talking about the job and the wife in the trailer home, I nod off against the window. Around 3:30, however, we stall on a deserted road in the middle of nowhere and have to hunt for wood to start a fire. Luckily, two headlights appear in the northern darkness within about fifteen minutes, and another truck gives us a boost.

In the morning the sun is shining on the snowy pines.

"This is my second wife," Nick says. "I killed the first one when I found out the slut was fucking around on me. I felt bad about killing the kid, though."

"You're not serious."

"I took them both out for a ride and rolled the car a few times to make it look like an accident. I don't think the little bastard was mine, anyway."

I don't really know what to say to him. A little later he tells me, "In this town where I lived, we used to pick up broads that were walking home or hitchhiking, and fuck them in the car." He grins, one eye glancing at me.

"You mean you raped them?"

"Aw, it wasn't rape, man, they loved it. We'd feed them whiskey and say, 'Give in or drink some more.' If they ever wanted to get out of the car they'd get smart, and if they didn't, well, they'd get so drunk they wouldn't know what was happening anyway."

"Well, if that's not rape it's kidnapping."

Nick puts his cigar in the ashtray and laughs. "We always had alibis. We'd just get the cops to call our friends, who'd tell them we were playing cards. They were out to nail me, boy. On Saturday night they'd ask me where I was going, and I'd tell them, 'To the policeman's ball, gentlemen.' I used to bootleg to the Indians, too. One time a couple of them didn't have the price of a bottle, so they gave me their twelve-year-old daughter instead."

I try to sleep some more with my head bouncing against the window, and the rumble of the truck in my ears. After I'm out for a few minutes, Nick slaps my knee. "Hey, look—there's a car stopped up the road." He pulls a flask from under the seat and unscrews the lid. "If there's just a broad in there we can fuck the ass off her."

"I'm not raping anyone."

"Relax."

He sucks back on the rye and gives it to me. I drink some, wondering how to handle him as he shifts down for our approach. It looks like a dirty blue Chev, and there's someone behind the wheel, all right.

"Holy shit," Nick enthuses. "This is *great*."

While we pass the car slowly, some old guy looks up at us.

"Goddamn it!"

"Don't you want to see if anything's wrong?"

"Ah, he's just jerking off." One eye glances at me, and the other one looks somewhere else.

At about four in the morning a few nights later, it hits me while I'm mucking around off that single rig, shovelling paths in the mud for water, breaking the ice and being deafened by machinery, how pure the snow is under billions of stars. We can spend our days reading comic books in the glare of a sun too radiant to invite introspection or melancholy, but frivolity departs with the descent of twilight. Our miserable human foibles mean nothing after dark.

When I look up into those heavens I know that I am gazing at the same moon which has fascinated aesthetes for thousands of years, that very goddess before whom writers, painters and poets have bowed throughout history. And even though this globe offers itself to every society wishing to pay homage, it feels like my personal bullion, and I know that I am the only one beholding it while standing in the snow and mud by that oil rig in the crisp air with the steel roaring and those voices shouting.

In this wild Canadian setting I think about life, death, suicide, destiny . . . The glory of the famous who kick off violently, and the infamy of those who killed them. Who I am, where I'm going, all of it.

When the job is finished I decide that I'm not going to sign up again. To hell with clamping on the slips and tongs, hosing down the oil and sawdust on the floor, the sixteen-hour shifts, the droning engines, the bastard tool pusher. I may leave Alberta and go on the road. Maybe head south.

In the meantime I'm sitting in a bar in Slave Lake with Colin, the derrick hand. He has to look for a job with a different outfit, having been fired for fighting with the driller in the dog-house. He pulls his tattered cowboy hat forward and rocks on his elbows, careful not to lean in the spilled beer, and asks, "Did I tell you about the guy who committed suicide by drilling five fuck-ing holes in his head? Jesus."

"Yeah." Raising my glass, I watch the Native Indians arguing behind him. A man and a big squaw both get to their feet while the boys at the pool table look over.

Colin turns as she punches the guy in the mouth and he sits down hard in his chair. Grinning his blackened teeth at me through his bristling moustache, he says, "She's a real scrapper, isn't she?"

"Sure is."

The woman says something to a little man in glasses beside her, then grabs him by the collar and lifts him up, banging his head against the wall. He just stares vacantly while sliding back down into his seat.

Through all the laughing and talking, a tune comes on the jukebox.

"That fucking honky tonk shit is driving me crazy," Colin says. Surprisingly, he likes classical music. "You know how some-times you get a song in your head that you can't get rid of? Once in a while it might be something incredible like Mozart, but mostly it's some awful, cocksucking bullshit."

Then he's talking about dentists. "' . . . Skip the fucking x-rays, Doc,' I told him. "Don't give me any fillings or any of that crap, just *yank* the buggers out.'" Colin takes a drag on his ciga-rette. "This civilization's going to collapse just like the Roman Empire."

The Indians at the next table are laughing. That squaw is quite the character. I momentarily fall in love with her in my drunken loneliness when she stands up and pulls her pants down for a couple of seconds. I actually swoon, then I start thinking about Verna.

Colin is smiling with his hat tilted over his eyes. "Another poor son of a bitch I heard about at this mill took off his glasses and watch, put them on the ground with his wallet, and jumped into a big chopper. He died of shock before he got diced like an egg, because he went in feet first. Jesus Christ, why don't they just change their names, run away, and pretend they're somebody else?"

21

I first smoked marijuana at thirteen with a British classmate and her friend at the back of a schoolyard. That same year I had a short story published in the yearbook about two girls who were axe-murdered in an English castle, then a poem profiling Jesus in the "Speak-Out" column of *The Toronto Telegram*, which paid five dollars.

I went through a suicidal phase the following year in grade nine, with emotional highs and lows from which I've never fully recovered. They were touched off by a multitude of seemingly innocuous things like minor slights, a smile from a pretty female. I bought myself a bottle of non-prescription sleeping pills and planned to kill myself, but seemed to reach a turning point one day in June over post-lunch cigarettes. We were watching girls from gym class race around the track when I announced, "And Ariel wins by a *tit*," which got quite a laugh, particularly from her boyfriend—our leader, more or less—who appreciated the compliment paid to her modest bosom. The sun appeared from behind a metaphorical cloud. Years later, he would choke to death on his vomit.

When I was sixteen I brought a girl home. We were having a polite conversation in the living room when my father, having once read a sexual episode in my journal, kept walking through and chaperoning with an angry expression. This was not only insulting to her, but it was becoming ludicrous, so we moved to the cellar steps. Then he decided he had things to do in the basement and started stomping up and down the stairs between us, driving me mad. Without telling anyone where we were going, I continued talking to her in the dark backyard, where she ended up giving me my first blowjob. So thanks, Dad.

In the summer of 1973 I hitchhiked across the country and down the coast to California. I had a place to stay in Oakland with the cousin of a classmate, up the street from the former Black Panther headquarters. There was an "Impeach Nixon" sign in their window. I also crashed in the San Anselmo home of a record industry executive at the invitation of his friend, a forty-one-year-old history graduate named Carl. We'd met in Washington in what we suspected was a stolen car driven by a knife-toting Latino, who also picked up a big Vietnam vet and three Germans, one of whom laughed when her boyfriend pulled off her bikini top in the back seat.

I dropped LSD for the first time with Carl on a grand stretch of beach outside San Francisco. Before I was properly off I noticed a girl walking along nude except for an open shirt, and admired her attitude so much that I removed all my clothes too, and went for a stroll California-style, at one with the universe. After she disappeared, I found that I was the only naked person anywhere. An elderly couple under big straw hats stared at me with their mouths ajar. But on I walked, getting increasingly stoned.

I was struck by the epiphany that my hallucinogenic trip was a metaphor for my cross-country journey: all roads had led to this moment. I was now a man. Then everything else became crystal clear as well. I must have gone close to a mile or so when I had to return to Carl to convey the splendor of a thousand insights which I had managed to summarize in a single, profound, magical sentence that I repeated over and over to myself while walking alongside the timeless ocean. Acid thundered over the surf as I happily tripped along by people who seemed to be politely ignoring my nudity. When I finally reached him, he smiled from another dimension, his eyes two pinwheels through the distortion of infrared rays. My phenomenal insight sounded slightly less staggering when I heard myself repeat it aloud to him. "You know," I said, "this really lays it all on the table."

(Izzy was dazzled by the aura of California LSD as once manufactured by the mythical chemist Owsley, and later persuaded me to sell him one of the two hits I mailed home for $5, double the standard price. Although I consider myself to be quite honest, I neglected to tell him that they'd been driven west from Ohio.)

On the route home I visited an aunt and uncle in Portland, Oregon where he worked for the police department analyzing drugs confiscated during arrests. One night he had to pick something up from the office and offered to show me around. Opening rows of cupboards packed with dope in labelled bags, he said, "This is marijuana. It's also called weed, pot or grass, and can be smoked in pipes or in cigarettes called 'joints'."

Although I was seventeen and had hair almost halfway down my back, Uncle Louis evidently believed in my innocence. After that, he unlocked cabinets to show me hash and cocaine. Since I planned to buy junk for the first time in Vancouver, I asked if he'd had any heroin arrests. He pulled out a drawer filled with H in cellophane bags identified by names, dates, and other details. "How," I inquired, "can you tell the quality?"

"We do a test similar to litmus paper experiments." He took a bag to the counter. "A type of acid's put on some of it, and the shade of purple it turns shows us the purity." After he applied a solution, I watched the powder change colour. "This is quite good by street standards."

"How does the average addict tell?"

"Well, heroin has a very bitter taste. Why don't you touch some to your tongue and then spit it out?"

I licked a fraction off my moistened finger, and after a moment wandered into the back room and snorted the rest. A faint tranquilizing effect. I asked if I might taste it again, then did the same thing while he was putting away his instruments. That time I became discernibly opiated and was answering in mono-syllables as I sat in a chair.

A couple of years later I was sorry to hear that their marriage broke up, he lost his job, and died shortly afterwards from a combination of alcohol and barbiturates.

In Vancouver, a woman to whom I'd given twelve dollars to buy and split a cap with me ripped me off. Once I did score and mainline heroin for the first time, I puked off the second floor porch of a house where people were dealing brown speed, and ended up crashing on a mattress lent to me by the junkie with whom I put in the money.

In the morning I was looking in a store window in the Gastown district when a fat guy about fifty-five in a dirty sweatshirt walked out of the mist, took the cap off his bald head, and said he wished he had hair like mine. I declined his offer to join him for a drink, but guess I felt sympathetic when he went on about how he just got off a freighter and didn't have anyone to talk to, and walked back with him to his fleabag hotel.

Clothes were strewn around the room. The window overlooked roofs, telephone wires, the side of a building painted with a 7–Up ad, and a sign for the nearby Savoy. Sitting on the bed, he said, "I can see in the windows over there, and watch the whores fucking their johns while I pull my cock."

"Where's that bottle?"

"On the boats everybody does it with everybody. There's no inhibitions or anything." He gave his crotch a tug. "So, are you an angel?"

"Yeah, I'm an angel."

"I had another guy in here who said he was, but when we were both on the bed together, I found out he wasn't any fucking angel."

At that point I told him that I was going to be on my way. He followed me to the door and said, "Some of my friends would give you a hard time right now if they were in my place. Do me a favour and go out the back way. I don't want the guy downstairs to see you leaving so soon."

I was skinny and he was built like a shithouse, so I went down the fire escape.

The following year, living at home again, I stayed in the city one long weekend instead of going up to the cottage with my parents, and invited a girl back from a barbecue early Sunday evening. We were naked in my room with a couple of beers when I heard a car door slam and realized that they'd come home a day early. It was only 7:30, so how was I going to explain being in bed? She was in a bit of a panic as well, so I put on my pants, trying to think what to do, and went out to the hallway to meet my father who was already coming up the stairs. Shielding my eyes from the light, I told him that I'd been drinking that afternoon with friends and went to bed early. He pushed into the doorway a few feet from the girl huddled on the bed around the corner, and grumbled that the room smelled like a goddamn brewery, and that I should stop wasting my life.

Afterwards, I gave her the choice of either getting dressed and the two of us walking out of the house right now, or else waiting until my parents went to sleep. She opted for the latter, and continued to rock and roll me until we tiptoed her out sometime after one.

Art should tell the truth within a creative structure. The trouble with many unknown artists is that they never butchered their ears. Once in an alley behind a bar, I was taking a leak against the wall while my friend was spelling his name on the ground, and he said, "It's too bad I can't piss paint."

At a job interview I had to explain why I thought I could be a copywriter, and said that I felt I was creative and had the artistic skills to better convey my ideas, whereas I should have professed a desire to manipulate the buying public. I've since come up with a variation of an old commercial: an executive jumps off a window ledge as the announcer blares, "He committed suicide, but his Samsonite briefcase held up," while it bounces on the concrete and the gutters are awash with blood.

The artist, deciding that there are no more boundaries to be overstepped, commits suicide as a final deviation from life itself . . .

22

I float into Great Falls, Montana and dump my gear on the hotel bed. Taking a pack of cigarillos from my coat, I light one and toss the match at my reflection in the old dresser mirror. I've grown my hair longer and am wearing it in a small ponytail. When I exhale, I look for the balance between the sissy my father once called me while kicking my ass on the floor, and the descendant of Reginald Fitz Urse, the son of a fucking bear and a legendary knight whose blood I surely possess.

It is February 1981.

In a hotel in Billings, Montana there is a chamber pot in the room, and a sign telling customers to empty it before leaving. A notice in the washroom down the hall says, "Don't Spit On Walls Or Floor."

In Idaho I get a ride with some Indians in an old Pontiac, and we drive across the snowy plains in twilight, a watercolour of pink and gray. Their baby girl shits her diapers while the sunset filters through a window bound with masking tape.

Idaho Falls: a couple of hotels I check out are booked up, so I go into a police station and ask if I might spend the night in jail, perhaps flirting with the mechanisms of justice in light of my assassination musings. They look at one another as if I'm something the cat dragged in, but decide it'll be all right and fill out a form listing my name, family's address, distinguishing marks, i.e., tattoos, then take my coat, gloves, tuque, scarf, knapsack, and the possessions in my pockets which they keep in a manila envelope.

A cop says he'll put me in the drunk tank, and escorts me down the hall to a room with beds and a table at which some perfectly sober men are silently playing cards. He unlocks the door and tells me quietly to yell if there's any kind of trouble. There are five whites and four Indians, but nobody answers when I say hello. A few of them are asleep. I find a bed, lie down, and drop off without hearing a word.

While I'm hitchhiking, a conversation with a driver gets around to John Lennon's death which isn't a subject I have a lot of patience for, considering all the bullshit I've heard about it—like how it ironically took a murder to bring everybody together, which would have made Lennon happy because love was what he was all about, etc.

This guy's potentially stupid comment is actually interesting however, when he says that the killer was such a big fan that the only way he could ever hope to impress himself on Lennon to the extent that Lennon had influenced him, was to actually shoot him. The true fanaticism of a disciple who wants to go beyond ripping a shirt or getting an autograph. Chapman had to pierce Lennon's heart the way the ex–Beatle had pierced his.

In Salt Lake City, Utah I lie on the top bunk in a mission. A tall cowboy is sprawled in the next bed with his hat between his feet. I hear snoring and coughing in the night while I amuse myself by contemplating the theoretical assassination of the President of the United States.

Maybe I've relinquished my morals in a jungle of violence which practices survival of the fittest, where something like one out of every four citizens owns a gun, a society in which immortality is achieved by killing or wounding important figures—if one considers Mark David Chapman, John Wilkes Boothe (Abraham Lincoln), Lee Harvey Oswald (John F. Kennedy), James Earl Ray (Martin Luther King), Sirhan Sirhan (Robert Kennedy), Arthur Bremner (attempted Governor George Wallace), and both the housewife and that Manson woman who on different occasions tried to blow away President Ford. Of course, if I forget their names it seems to contradict my thesis, doesn't it?

Conspiracy theories aside, the assassin is the new anti–hero. While my father wouldn't be proud of me, at least he'd know that

I had the courage to commit a significant act and that I wasn't destined for mediocrity. My face would be on the cover of *Time*, which gets delivered to his door every week. Well, if it wasn't featured out front, it would certainly be inside, and the old man would have a famous son.

In the morning there is a long line to the washroom across from my bed. The can has a toilet and sink but no door. Some of the hobos void their bowels while the crowd awaits the wiping of their asses, one by one.

We assemble on the sidewalk outside the kitchen in the bitter darkness as elderly men spit on the sidewalk and lean in doorways. I am talking with a Hispanic, who out of the blue, asks for a buck or two. Although I have some traveller's cheques and cash, there is no reason for this punk to assume that I have much more than a dollar, so the idea that I'd hand over everything is a slander on my character. I take comfort from the thought that this fucking wetback is going to see my picture on the cover of *Newsweek* and realize that I was nobody to piss off.

Kansas City spans the borders of Kansas and Missouri, so maybe they're separate towns, I don't know. I'm crossing the bridge above some railway tracks under a cloudy sky, looking at boxcars and "The Colombian Steel Tank Co./Sheet Steel Fabricator" before walking up a street alongside "Kans. City Bolt, Nut and Screw." I pause to observe a fire-gutted hotel before checking into another dive at $4 per night.

Later, I make my way to a strip of red and purple cocktail lounges with pink doors and neon lights, and go into one that advertises: "Rendezvous For Good Drinks/Live/Go-Go and Exotic/Noon Until 1 A.M./Continuous Entertainment/Now Appearing Nitely." The sign is badly painted and features a blonde in a red bikini and high heels.

Inside, I order a beer and talk to this disoriented black who chatters off his head and tells every passing woman, "Hey, Mama, get down."

Pondering my socio-political theories, I reason that Reagan is elderly so it wouldn't be like I'd be cutting him down in the prime of life. To shoot him would almost be an act of kindness since he'd achieve all that media coverage and immortality when he's ready to pop off from natural causes anyway, and they'd probably be more compassionate towards him in the history books. I once saw him in a movie called *She's Working Her Way Through College* with an actress named Virginia Mayo, and he seemed pleasant enough. It's nothing personal.

I believe in capital punishment although I'm appalled by the methods of execution. Frying a man in the electric chair while his eyeballs jump from their sockets and his blackened flesh sizzles is torture by any criteria. I'm dumfounded that such a sloppy and gruesome contraption could be accepted by modern society. The sensibility is something out of the middle ages.

Hanging isn't instantaneous, nor do I think is lethal injection, although both are preferable to such past methods as boiling, burning, dismembering, crucifying or burying alive. In India during the rule of the Rajahs, elephants were forced to drag culprits through the streets before stepping on their heads. Not a circus trick. Overlooking the ignominious departure of head from body, the guillotine may be the most humane practice.

While I understand arguments promoting the salvation of killers, when all is said and done, they simply under-value the suffering of victims. Forget the low instinct of revenge, the compounded angst of the condemned having to wait for death, the fact that execution makes society equally guilty of murder, and so on. Those opposing capital punishment don't elevate the value of an existence, they reduce it to the equivalent of a prison term. (I am a hypocrite, advocating abortion.)

The obvious solution tempering justice with humanity in cases of first degree murder is to offer a choice of options by which to die unnaturally, including three drinks with your last meal. But fast—no lingering on death row. As a convicted assassin I would choose the firing squad. But even that smacks of unnecessary drama, and I suspect that you'd feel a punctured heart before bleeding to death. No, I'd take a blindfold and a bullet in the head.

When I watch the show in this bar, I can't help but find it interesting that strippers usually make their audience sit through rock. Now Dads are only too happy to hear music they wouldn't tolerate at home.

I don't think men can become women by transsexual surgery and estrogen treatments, for I'm convinced there's a delicacy to females that no male can approximate whatever his degree of femininity. I worship their distinction.

Nature dictates that a man subconsciously feel that he's mastering a woman during intercourse by the posture of sex itself, for she becomes physically receptive even if she's otherwise dominant. His erection is the active factor on which penetration hinges.

One can see this underlying theme in copulation by the deviation of the sex killer who goes beyond the figurative act of piercing by dismembering females altogether and probing their apparatuses. An already questionable system goes awry. Who can say what motivates a woman? We're sufficiently sophisticated to realize it's not always blind love, a sense of duty or maternal ambitions. She guards her mystery, she knows its value, she lures males with a calculated dance.

And yes, I'm still thinking about Verna.

When I leave, I try to pick up a black woman on the street. I don't have an intelligent line or any kind of excuse for talking to her, I just say, "Please forgive the approach, but can I buy you a drink somewhere?"

If looks could kill. "*What?*"

"I asked if I could buy you a drink."

"No!"

This attracts the attention of a couple of blacks on the corner, so Whitey keeps walking. ("They've got some crazy little women there/ And I'm going to get me one.")

The next day I get KANSAS CITY tattooed beneath my Saturn. I am a universal vagabond.

23

In red-dirt Oklahoma under blue skies, a dark Buick sedan with a white roof pulls over for me. The driver is an attractive woman in her early thirties with short brown hair, aviator sunglasses, a tank top and jeans. Fairly wholesome looking, friendly, articulate, minimal make-up. During the course of conversation, I am somewhat surprised when she tells me that she's a working girl from a cathouse outside Las Vegas, on her way home to visit her parents.

She has a hate-on for pimps, who it seems important that I understand, are almost always black. The stereotype is accurate. Before she joined the ranch they were always pressuring her to work for them. When one slapped her around and tried to rip her off, she shot him in the stomach. Although he survived and is now in jail, a magazine doing a story on prostitution dubbed her "The Pimp Killer."

I ask her what she considers the wildest request every made of her in the business. After thinking about it for a moment, she wants to know if I'm including oral sex, presumably to determine just how ignorant I am, then tells me that an elderly regular used to come in with a knife and fork, and pay the girls to piss in a glass and shit on a plate. He got his kicks by drinking and eating it.

Although I have the cash I'm not much into prostitution, being essentially motivated by a sense of mutual attraction. I try to cut through the red tape by telling her that I'd certainly buy her favours if I could afford them, but she smiles tolerantly and says that money talks and bullshit walks.

I have a dream that I'm washing my clothes in a gas station toilet bowl, flushing to rinse . . .

The future always seems to emerge in conceptual design as a point, the way corners are cut in cars and architecture as if our understanding will narrow to finite dimensions when life becomes clear.

In a bar a few years ago when I was stoned on LSD, I wondered: if you get into a scrap with someone who revolts you, are you repelling their putrid existence or inadvertently embracing it?

One night during another acid trip I saw a beautiful butterfly illuminated by a street light on a store window. When I cautiously approached it for a better look, I discovered that it was, in fact, a horribly colourful gob of spit.

I associate the north with the exterior in that one might experience blizzards, gangrened flesh or death from exposure, whereas the south is interior: disease, Montezuma's Revenge, poisonous bites. A deceptive beauty whose evil works within.

In the Lone Star State the sun seems falsely comforting given that murder is everywhere in America, and there is always a chance that my head could end up in a garbage can. I spend my first night in Houston in a Salvation Army, before floating further downtown the following morning to get myself a room in a flophouse hotel.

While I'm paying my eight bucks, a couple of hookers sashay through the dingy lobby, and the large desk clerk congenially informs me that I've got myself a room at the biggest whorehouse in the city. Closing the register, he comes around the counter and explains that he doesn't have a spare key to give me, and will have to go upstairs to open my door. In the ancient elevator I notice a knife on the box by the lever. As we walk down the dim hallway he can't find my key on his chain either, and ends up picking my lock with the blade.

Putting my gear down, I look over the ruins: torn shade, plywood over a broken window, dirty peeling paint, bare light bulb, overhead fan which revolves slowly when I pull the string.

Early that afternoon I'm sitting in a coffee shop when a tall, sharply dressed brother of about thirty-five slowly walks over and sits down at my table. "Hey," he drawls, taking off his shades. Although he's under the influence of something, his dilated pupils indicate that it's not junk.

I'm suspicious of people approaching me for no apparent reason, because they're usually panhandlers, homosexuals, religious freaks, or trying to unload questionable drugs. He seems offended, even oddly hurt by my lack of warmth, and says, "I only sat down because you looked cool, bro."

Well, I don't know about that, but I am disarmed enough to say hello. "Otis," he tells me, giving me a noncommittal shake. It only seems polite to introduce myself as well, and find myself pushing my fries towards him as I finish my grilled cheese sandwich.

We talk about nothing in particular. He doesn't seem to be in a hurry to state his business or go anywhere. After five or ten minutes, however, he suggests hunting for some women and maybe setting me up with a girlfriend or two if we run into any of them on the street. If that's the angle, he hasn't mentioned money.

We leave the restaurant and go for a walk.

"I got a stomach ache," he says. "Let's get us a beer, all right?"

We stop in a bar. I'm rather enjoying his company, actually, and begin calling him Shaft. He seems amused that I still appear to doubt his motives, but doesn't hold it against me, and suggests buying a couple of bottles of wine if we find some girls.

Then we continue our prowl under the Texas sun.

Otis checks out a sidewalk display and decides to buy a hat. He picks up a white straw number and puts it on, tilting the brim, then goes inside to pay for it. When he comes back out we keep walking, but he complains about his stomach again, then stops and doubles over in pain. He doesn't look very well.

"What is it?" I ask.

"I'm . . . sick, man. I've gotta go home."

A bus pulls over to the curb. I didn't realize we were standing by the stop. With barely another word, he gets on, and is gone.

Here are the facts about my ancestor, Reginald Fitz Urse:

King Henry II didn't like the separation of church from state which allowed something called Benefit of Clergy, where clerks could only be tried by ecclesiastical courts for crimes other than misdemeanors and high treason. Consequently, they could escape punishment for such things as robbery, rape and murder.

Henry became friendly with the Archdeacon of Canterbury, Thomas à Becket, and appointed him the Chancellor of England in 1154 when Becket was thirty-seven. In 1162, a year following the death of the former Archbishop of Canterbury, the King offered Thomas the post. Becket treated this as a joke and warned him against it, but Henry insisted.

Immediately afterwards, Becket sent in his resignation as the chancellor, wore a haircloth, lived on vegetables, grain and water, and washed the feet of thirteen beggars every night. Henry was stunned that his pal had become a nasty opponent, and conflicts about minor things led to the predictable hassle over clergy privileges. Becket insisted that only for a second offense could the civil courts try a man who had been ordained.

The King assembled the knights and bishops of England in 1164 and persuaded them to sign the Constitutions of Clarendon, which ended many clerical immunities. By one account Becket weakened and gave his consent, although he was ashamed afterwards and welcomed trouble over the archbishop's estates in Sussex to stir it up again. By another he wouldn't give the documents his seal. In either case, Henry put the new laws into effect and accused Thomas of feudal disobedience. Becket refused to listen to this and said that he'd appeal to the Pope, threatening to excommunicate anyone who agreed to the trial, and walked out of the room despite orders for his arrest.

That evening he fed some poor people in his London home and by night escaped in disguise across the channel to find shelter in a monastery in St. Omer in the jurisdiction of the King of France. Pope Alexander III defended his stand but sent him to live as a Cistercian monk in the abbey of Pontigny.

Henry II banished Becket's relatives from England and threatened to confiscate the property of all priories in Britain, Normandy, Anjou and Aquitaine connected with the abbey of Pontigny if its abbot continued to let Becket stay, so the abbot begged Becket to leave, and he lived for a while on alms in a cheap inn at Sens.

Louis VII of France prodded the Pope into commanding Henry to restore Becket to his former position or face an interdict of all religious services in the English territories. The King went to Avranches in 1170, met Becket and promised to fix things. The archbishop returned triumphantly to Canterbury on December 1st, where he was welcomed home by the crowds. He managed the excommunications of the Archbishop of York and the Bishops of London and Salisbury, so the three went to France to complain to Henry, who was still there.

He got pissed off by the whole business and said, "Shall a man who has eaten my bread . . . insult the King and all the kingdom, and not one of the lazy servants whom I nourish at my table does me right for such an affront?"

So herein lies your fame, dear ancestor:

Interpreting these words, you and three other knights— Hugh de Morville, William de Tracy and Richard le Breton— crossed the channel, and by conflicting reports arrived in Canterbury Dec. 29th or 30th, forced your way into Becket's chambers during dinner, and had a big argument over the excommunications.

(In T.S. Eliot's play, the fourth knight identified you to the audience as the leader, while the third knight referred to you as an old friend. You were pretty well regarded, Fitz Urse, you bold Saxon motherfucker.)

Becket wouldn't listen and you left, but returned an hour later armed to the teeth. Monks barricaded the house and dragged the archbishop into the church. Becket wouldn't let them turn it into a fortress, however. You pushed through the crowd and met up with him in the chapel where he'd placed himself by a pillar in the north transept. All his companions had gone except for one man whose arm was broken trying to defend him. You and the boys cut Thomas à Becket down with swords and marched back through the people, your moment in the black sun.

The King stayed in his chambers and refused food for three days, then sent word to the Pope declaring his innocence. He rescinded the Constitutions of Clarendon and restored all previous rights and property of the church. As to what happened to you, accounts differ. One book said that you and the other knights escaped overseas and no attempt was made to bring you to justice, while another claimed that Henry II ordered your arrest.

Becket was canonized, the church proclaimed him a saint in 1172, and soon thousands were making pilgrimages to his shrine. Henry undertook the journey some years later, walking the last three miles on bare, bleeding feet. He got down before Becket's tomb and persuaded the monks to whip him. Thomas' shrine stood for more than three hundred years as a record of the triumph of the church over state until Henry VIII had it destroyed and the martyr's bones scattered. Benefit of Clergy was on the statute book until 1827.

Back at the hotel, the greasy clerk interrupts his conversation with a couple of reprobates hanging around the desk to take me up to my room. In the elevator he discovers that the knife has been stolen, so after we walk down the hall, he steps back and *kicks* my door open. I forget if this place has three stars or four.

When I check the lock, it somehow still seems to work. I thank him, and as he starts to leave I invite him into the room for a moment to discuss something. The clerk looks a bit surprised, and glances down the hall as he follows me inside. I turn on the light and close the door behind him. "I'm travelling these days, and was just wondering if you might know where I could pick up a gun. For protection."

He hooks his hair behind his ear with his thumb, squinting. The majority of the tattoos on his arms are of the jailhouse variety. "Well, there's a pawn shop a couple of blocks over, but there's a waiting period . . ." He pauses, thinking something over as he looks at me. "Maybe I could give you a deal myself on a twenty-two. A hundred bucks, with some bullets."

I'm not sure what the logistics of buying a gun with an unknown history are, so I ask, "Wouldn't you be on the hook if I shot somebody with a gun registered to you?"

"Between the two of us, it's hot. You can kill whoever the hell you want."

I consider it. "Would you take seventy-five?"

"Ninety, and that's the lowest."

"All right."

After the clerk leaves to get it, I pull the string to turn on the fan, and pace the room. It's hard to believe that I'm more than halfway there. I look out the window at the poor, sunlit district. When he returns, he takes a mean-looking little piece from under his T-shirt and hands it to me. As I look it over, he pulls seven bullets out of his pockets and sits down on the bed under the whirling blades. When he asks if I've ever handled one, I tell him the truth, and he runs through the basic operation for me.

Later, I aim it at the window by the plywood, sighting along the short barrel, and consider the risk of various murders being traced to this gun. I guess it won't make much difference after the shooting. To be honest, I'm not sure I'm completely serious about the idea, but it does seem to be moving ahead. The .22 is now a reality which feels capable of altering destinies.

24

Back in grade eleven, my gym teacher was angered by my indifference and told me to quit school.

Next year, irascible Mrs. Rhodes who taught English denounced me as a failure before the class. I was calm in the face of her delirium and asked her to explain herself. When she retorted that I was apathetic, I produced a history essay for which I'd just received an A+. "I didn't say you weren't intelligent," she answered. "I'm saying you've got a bad attitude." Well, this didn't constitute failure by my understanding; rather, I took it as a compliment.

As for others whose paths I've crossed—

In the course of breaking into an apartment, an ex-schoolmate named Sid was surprised by the occupants and took the woman hostage at knifepoint, sexually assaulting her in his car. The media quoted a psychiatrist who called him a walking time bomb. Although it was unanimously agreed that he was mentally disturbed, he was nonetheless tried as sane since he realized the difference between right and wrong.

Four people I knew were killed in car crashes. One of them, a guy named Warman, was intrigued by my first tattoo and asked if it hurt. I told him, "I bit a bullet, asshole."

"You bit a bullet's *asshole*?"

A woman down the street asphyxiated herself in the garage after she discovered her husband hanging beside the furnace.

Someone I had a small altercation with in junior high was in the newspaper for kicking a policeman in the mouth in a hospital, where he had been taken en route to the station after a bar fight.

An acquaintance with whom I once hit junk spent inconse-
quential time in jail for drug offenses until he put on a ski mask
to hold up the milk store across the street with a kitchen knife.
Despite the fact that he was recognized by the clerk and told to
go home, he persisted and was consequently sent up for armed
robbery. After getting out he was involved in a substantial heroin
seizure and is now doing hard time.

My only encounter with Mario took place in grade two.
Bobby and Doug said he could probably beat me up, to which I
shamefully retorted that I could run faster. He was recently
acquitted of the first degree murder of his pregnant wife; don't ask
me why. The police were suspicious of his claim that intruders
broke in since a shotgun death was inconsistent with burglary, and
then discovered the weapon in a false ceiling in his basement.
Despite letters from girlfriends that the prosecution provided for
a motive, the jury was unconvinced.

I used to baby-sit a likable if rambunctious boy named Billy.
One evening he and his brother ran around the street in their
underwear. When I got one into the house, the other would
escape out the back door. Once in their room they threw all their
toys out the window, and sent paper airplanes down to their
cheering friends. When Billy was a teenager he became a patient
in mental wards and threatened to kill his father, tried to burn
down the house while everyone slept, and ended up hanging
himself with a bed sheet in a psychiatric hospital.

A manic little character from my high school gym class
named Marty has since become a famous stand-up comedian and
TV actor in a highly acclaimed American series. I've watched him
interviewed by Johnny Carson. I have no poignant anecdotes. I
want to transcend his summit and be known in China, Italy and
New Zealand, independent of public or critical support. Enter
history through the alley with my .22.

I try to live by a standard of self-realization set by a high
school teacher who, after suffering a nervous breakdown, came to
terms with his limitations by drawing up a method by which stu-
dents started the year with 100 and worked their way down, their
grades clearly self-determined and thus no responsibility of his. As

he marked my notebook he deducted a point for ink blots on the back cover, quietly refusing my explanation. They constituted a breach of neatness however well organized. His eyes were dull and he never raised his voice, perhaps due to tranquilizers. I admired his sense of calm, medically imposed or otherwise.

A girl I know once passed out on the living room couch at a party, later got up in a daze, went behind the sheer curtains at the picture window, pulled her pants down in front of everyone, and urinated on the floor. She then wiped herself with the drapes and stumbled back to the sofa. Another time she got drunk in a restaurant and wove her way towards the ladies' room, but bumped into a table which had just been served, vomited on the meals, fell down, and had to be pushed outside in a wheelchair.

People are often convinced that their true selves consist of those insecurities uprooted in dreams and psychoanalysis, without realizing that the strengths they overlook comprise their personalities as well.

It's a bitter irony that one reaches one's physical prime at the outset of adulthood, not unlike June 21st being the longest day of the year—summer is still before us, yet the season is already in decline. How unfair it seems that all those bald or varicose-veined people in their forties have such a lengthy plummet to death ahead of them.

Aren't journalists would-be gods with their superior perceptions and dictums, etc.? Despite their re-creations of life and the manipulation of language, however, they are not artists. Supportive or critical of the establishment, they are safe within its structure.

One of my paranoias is that optometrists deliberately over-prescribe to keep the world myopic, for how often have they said that a person's eyes will adjust to new lenses, suggesting that one's sight needs to deteriorate to accommodate the glasses? Children become forever dependent.

If a writer describes a sunset as viewed by his characters, the reader will gloss over it rather than taking the time to conjure beauty these people have already sullied with their presence.

Last winter I phoned a few people regarding a speed party, and gave Mark a call. (This being the juvenile delinquent in the trademark blond wig from earlier tales, who went on to spend time in reform school and jail.) He said he was looking for junk, but if he had no luck by eleven P.M. he'd contribute some money. I didn't hear from him.

The events of the following night as later described by Terri, his common law wife:

Mark, herself, our friend Izzy, and a woman named Gloria hit up at 7:30 P.M. Terri vomited intermittently for the rest of the evening, while Mark mainlined two more times. Terri and Izzy carried him to the bedroom around 1:00 A.M. His snoring woke her up at 2:30, and she rolled him out of bed onto the floor. She awakened at 4:00 thinking that someone, perhaps her five-year-old daughter, had called her name.

In the morning she tried to rouse Mark who was lying face-down on the ground, and found him very heavy when she turned him over. She called for assistance and gave him mouth-to-mouth resuscitation. He hadn't pissed or shit himself, but when they pumped his chest he spewed some kind of stinking liquid into Gloria's face.

The three carried him outside, accidentally dropping him into a snow bank before the ambulance arrived.

The doctor at the hospital said he died of a heroin overdose around 4:00, which made Terri crazy, wondering if he'd called out for her. She demanded to know why Izzy didn't suspect anything since he'd apparently seen an OD or two before. Gloria told the police what happened, and Izzy was charged with manslaughter for having provided the lethal dosage, though Terri got him off the hook by claiming that Mark did another fix unbeknownst to him before they came over.

She clutched his hand in the funeral home, bawling, "That's not him, that's not him," and then later in the church, when the service began without her, grabbed the priest by the arm as he was walking by her pew and cried, "Who the hell am I, goddamnit? Do you think I'm *nobody*? His family never cared! You should've waited for me!" I was sitting behind her and saw that she was blurred by Valiums again, her face streaked with tears.

A few weeks later, Terri was revived in the hospital from a barbiturate overdose.

After a couple of months I went out with her for a while. She'd regained her cynical humour and told me that a subway driver had once sprayed her with a fire extinguisher when she wouldn't put out her cigarette, and that she'd prostituted herself working in a massage parlor on Yonge Street. Also, that she and Mark used to fight a lot but it didn't mean anything. He bought her a ring and they were going to get married. A few times he punched her ribs so badly that she got prescriptions for Percodans from which he removed the buffer for mainlining. (I subsequently learned to do the same thing with her later prescriptions.) On another occasion she fell asleep during sex, and he finished it off by masturbating on her face.

Terri had hard good looks, but her figure was slowly going to hell. I stopped her from stealing glasses from bars in my attempt to explain to her the difference between right and wrong, although she claimed to be teaching me the opposite.

25

I thumb east in a route that I figure will eventually lead to Washington, D.C., where the source of my fame awaits me. I talk with strangers about the President and look at newspapers to see if he is scheduled to travel anywhere. As a descendant of Reginald Fitz Urse, I like to tell myself that if I go through with it I am upholding the family name. Murder is the worst crime of course, but political violence has had support from such famous people in history as Thomas Jefferson, who supposedly said that the United States should have a revolution every twenty years.

Louisiana: Cajun, bayous, zydeco, cypresses, swamps. I hitch-hike past Lake Charles and Lafayette to Baton Rouge, where I watch freighters in the Mississippi, which is flowing south towards the Gulf of Mexico.

By evening I'm standing by the side of the road a few miles outside New Orleans. A VW Beetle pulls over in a flurry of dust and gravel, and I run towards it. "Thanks," I say, climbing in.

"Sure." The driver gives me a nervous glance and then looks away, shifts gears, and we're off again.

He's fairly nondescript, in his early to mid-thirties, light curly hair. When we start talking, I notice he has what I've heard referred to as that Brooklynesque N'Awlins accent. On the out-skirts of the city the conversation takes a turn when he says, "We have alot of bars here. Quite a few gay ones too." He taps his hand on the wheel. "I go to them sometimes."

After a silence, he feels the need to clarify: "Yeah, sometimes I blow and give hand jobs to guys under the tables."

I watch the scenery in the dusk as we enter the town of the Mardi Gras. Well, it's been months since I've been with a woman, and if there's anything I've regretted about my experience in the construction camp, it was not charging Victor any money on principle.

The guy clears his throat. "I guess that disgusts you. Fags and everything."

"It doesn't mean anything to me."

With a quick glance, he asks, "Would you like me to, um, give you a blowjob or maybe jack you off?"

"Well . . . I might let you blow me, but I could really use some cash."

"How much?"

I'm such a dumb-ass hustler that I haven't any idea, and mutter, "Fifteen bucks."

"What?"

Louder, I tell him, "Twenty bucks."

If he picked up the difference, he doesn't say. "All right, but I don't have that much on me. I have to go to a friend's place to get it. Is that okay? He doesn't live that far."

He takes a detour. We drive through a residential neighbourhood until he pulls into the driveway of an older, two-storey wooden house. There is a porch and a small front yard with a flowerbed and bushes. He shifts into park, then turns off the engine and looks at me with a tentative smile. "I bet they'd love to meet you. Why don't we go into the bedroom where it'll be more comfortable?"

"No, it's in the front seat or nothing."

He goes inside. It's fairly dark now. I look along the street at the lighted windows, the trees, and a cat on someone's verandah. After a few minutes the guy gets back in and turns the ignition, driving the VW further into the shadows. When I pull down my pants and underwear, he goes for my prick like a dog going for a bone, and I have to ask him to lighten up the way I had to with Victor. In fact, he's also rubbing his crotch through his pants and asking me to let him know when I'm going to come, presumably so we can ejaculate in harmony.

Afterwards, he opens the car door and spits out my semen with a breathless apology. "I'm sorry, but I can't swallow spunk. It makes me sick."

The guy gives me twenty-five instead. Perhaps he was out cruising or not going much farther, because he drives me half a mile to a major intersection where he says I can catch a ride downtown. I appreciate the gesture of the extra five dollars, but when he asks to meet again the next day, I have to decline.

Later that night I check into a mission on Camp Street for $1.50. They give me a number, and I climb the staircase to a large, dimly lit room with rows of beds. There are plaster walls, a sink and mirror, exposed wooden joists in the ceiling. Off to the side, I notice a washroom with showers and open stalls.

A big, bare-chested black man with long sideburns and a Fu Manchu moustache is sitting nearby with two whites. "Well, look what we got here," he mutters in a deep voice, taking a swig of wine.

Unhappily, I realize that he's sitting on the bed I've been assigned. When I put down my gear and say hello, he asks, "This yours?"

"Yeah."

"Here, man." He hands me the bottle, which I raise to my dry mouth. "I'm Frank. This here's Luke and Tony. Where you from?"

He watches me with his right eye while I introduce myself. The other one seems to be glass.

Luke brushes his wavy blond hair straight back, a cigarette between two fingers. Motherfucker has sleepy blue eyes, high cheekbones, a multitude of tattoos, and a cross of nails around his neck. "Well, I've been everywhere, and I can tell you that the most fucked up people are here in New Orleans."

"Bullshit," Frank snorts, passing the wine. "It's easy to see you ain't been to New York."

"Is that where you're from?" I ask.

"Yeah."

Tony's eyes are in shadow until he tilts his head to drink. His balding scalp shines under the light, and I notice a scar along his mouth. When he surrenders the bottle, he says to the others, "Hal was over there sucking everybody off, and he told me he wanted to be my slave."

Luke takes a drag. "So he loves you."

"My boyfriend here's cuter than Hal," Frank says with a nod in my direction.

I take a drink and ignore the compliment.

"You working on that garbage truck tomorrow?" Tony asks.

Frank holds up a bandaged thumb. "No, this prick is still killing me."

When the bottle's finished, Tony thumps it against the floorboards. "You sorry buggers coming to the bar?"

Luke drops the smoldering filter and crushes it with his boot.

"My man and me are going to make love," Frank says. "I'm going to get more wine." He turns to me as he puts on a shirt. "You'll be up for a while, right?"

"No, I'm going to sleep."

They drop the empty bottle in the garbage can and head down the creaking stairs. I take off my shoes and shirt and push my knapsack under the bed, then get beneath the covers with my pants on. It's a long way from Starbuck Island.

As I lie there looking up at the timbers, I wonder if I should leave and find a cheap hotel, then root through my things to check the gun. Nobody else seems to be awake, so I turn off the remaining light.

I pretend to be asleep when I hear footsteps on the staircase. Frank shakes me as he comes in, and says in a low voice, "Hey, I got the wine." He sits down on his bed, which is next to mine, and unscrews the lid. His face is lit by the window. "Honey, don't go to sleep on me now."

"I'm tired."

He sucks back on the bottle and wipes his mouth. "Here—I hate to drink alone."

I slowly sit up and take it.

"Babe, you know in this life I don't believe anything's wrong if it doesn't do nobody any harm. You know what I mean?" He accepts the wine. "I believe in pleasure. That's why I live. Sex and drinking are my fucking loves, man."

"I'm straight, so you're wasting your time."

"Honey, you're so pretty." Frank takes a swig, and seems to wink. "How come your lips are so red?"

I smile as I take the bottle. "Because I've been drinking this shit."

"We're all of us both male and female together, and you know, I think you're about sixty percent girl. Sugar, don't fight it."

A match flares, and he lights a cigarette. The medallion around his neck glints and disappears into darkness. "Why, I'd swear you were a girl."

"Tell me about New York."

"Fuck New York."

"Where's Luke from?"

"Las Vegas." A red glow cuts through the air as Frank rests a hand on his leg and exhales. He swallows some wine and hands the bottle over. "I want to tell you about your womanly ways."

"Fuck my womanly ways. How did you hurt your thumb?"

He looks at me, then sighs. "I'll tell you if you don't bug me no more about it." Turning his head, he says, "See the stitches back there where my hair's shaved off? Well, that's from the same robbery that fucked up."

I take a contemplative drink.

Frank breaks the silence. "I've known some strange people . . . Man, this dude in New York was so black he was blue. He walked the streets of Harlem wearing a loincloth with all this coloured shit painted on his face like he was on the warpath or something. Crazy . . . But the real trouble's the stupid brothers like Chester over there who don't know fuck-all about their heritage." He nods to a bed up the aisle as he reaches for the bottle. "Just another dumb nigger who doesn't know *shit* about Africa."

"So, how'd you end up here? What did you used to do?"

He seems to raise an eyebrow. "I once made up a saying that a fool can ask more questions in a minute than a wise man can answer in a lifetime. I was a boxer, if you've got to know."

"What class?"

Leaning forward, he smiles and says in a low voice, "Look, I know your problem. "*I'll* do the passive thing. I'll suck your cock and lick the freckles off your back. You won't believe what I'll do for you. I'll bite your toenails and lick your feet. Baby, it'll be so good. I'll do anything because I just want to make it with you. I'll lick your asshole so you'll swear you were in Heaven."

I laugh softly but am careful not to insult him. "Listen, you're a good looking guy. Why don't you get yourself a girlfriend? You could do well for yourself."

"Man . . ." He sits back and flicks his ash. "I was an ugly kid. Anyway, I'm a confirmed homosexual. You're just trying to make old Frank suffer, aren't you? You're a fuckin' tease because you know you're pretty. You got nothing to lose by trying it."

I figure it's best to dissuade him from an angle which could keep the conversation going all night, and say, "Look, it so happens that a guy paid me twenty-five dollars to blow me on the way over here, so it's not that I don't know anything about it."

He goes back on one elbow and studies me in the semi-darkness. "Oh, so *that's* it. How much do you want?"

"Nothing. It's just that I was broke. I brought it up to show you that only under a circumstance like that would I ever do that kind of thing. It's nothing personal."

Frank butts his cigarette and reaches under his pillow. My heart skips a beat when he pulls out a long knife and thrusts it towards me. "Take it," he whispers roughly. "Take it and *kill* me. I can't go through this no more. Put me out of my fucking misery. I swear you're trying to drive me *insane*."

He tosses it on the bed, and with a swing of his arm throws an imaginary rope over a beam. Catching his throat with his hand and tilting back his head, he gasps, "Hang me by the neck until I'm dead. Lord, don't make me suffer no more!"

I am relieved, but don't give him any satisfaction. Although I almost feel guilty, it doesn't seem natural for such a big black son of a bitch to act the female without trying to fuck me once my pants are down. I have a gun which theoretically makes me just as dangerous, but it might not be proper etiquette to hold it on him while he's giving me head.

26

The news is everywhere: President Ronald Reagan has been shot. They say that White House Press Secretary James Brady died with a bullet through his brain (though he in fact survives), and it seems that a Secret Service agent named Timothy McCarthy was hit in the stomach, but is reportedly doing well. A Washington D.C. policeman named Thomas Delhanty was shot in the shoulder and neck, but his condition is stable.

Ronald Reagan is in the hospital, and I gather through all the confusion that his health is going to be okay.

The botched assassination attempt happened outside the Washington Hilton where the President had addressed a few thousand union representatives in the International Ballroom, and now everyone is hearing about America's newest shooting star.

John Hinckley is twenty-five like myself, and also has a fair complexion. He is the son of wealthy parents in Colorado, and has an older sister who was very popular and somewhat overshadowed him.

He is said to be soft-spoken and Protestant, and apparently wasn't a troublesome teenager or even a loner. In grades seven and eight he managed the basketball team, and while in high school was a member of the civic affairs club. As a senior he was in the rodeo club, and seemed very happy.

Once away from home at Texas Tech in 1973, Hinckley made no effort to socialize. He was a business major for a while, but later dropped out in favour of a liberal arts program. He was at school for seven years, attending classes more than half the time, although he didn't graduate and never spoke in class.

The guy was a member of the National Socialist Party of America for more than a year between 1978–'79, and marched in a Nazi parade in St. Louis, although they kicked him out for promoting violence, as this aroused their suspicions that he was either a nut or a federal agent.

Of course, the newspapers light upon his unfortunate love life and discover his infatuation with the actress Jody Foster, to whom he wrote letters and cherished in the movie *Taxi Driver*. Hinckley yearned to shoot Reagan in an effort to win her love, although she never encouraged his attention let alone advocated that he do this for her benefit.

It appears that our anti-hero stepped off a Greyhound in Washington, D.C. after a three-day ride from L.A., and checked into the Park Central Hotel. People recalled later that he was nervous on the sidewalk before he pointed his Saturday night special at the President and shot twice, then paused and fired off four more rounds. Secret Service agents and police officers and even a union representative jumped on him. He was handcuffed and a jacket was thrown over his head before he was tossed into a cruiser.

His gun was filled with devastator bullets which were designed to explode on contact, something like dumdums. They apparently cost twelve times as much as ordinary .22 slugs, but most of them failed to blow up.

I read that the Treasury Department's Bureau of Alcohol, Tobacco and Firearms discovered within minutes that Hinckley had purchased his pistol at a certain pawn shop in Dallas, so that if he'd escaped, the FBI would have had his identity anyway.

Isn't it interesting the way we're both twenty-five-year-old Protestant drifters who bought .22s in Texas? If it was more than a shattered thought on my part and I had in fact shot Reagan, the magazines would have relegated me to their junkyards of psycho-analytical jargon the way they discussed Arthur Bremner's romantic humiliations, Hinckley's passion for Foster, and James Earl Ray's prostitutes. They'd dig up the hooker I met at the Warwick Hotel, my voodoo chile Verna, and maybe even Victor and the other guy who went down on me in New Orleans, and write or imply that I was incapable of a satisfying relationship with a female of my own race—ignoring my other romances which probably meet some level of statistical acceptability, even if they weren't long term.

And they'd mention my tattoos which no doubt compensate for some emotional deficiency. My dear emblems render me artistic, and I'm not just talking a vicarious creative experience; I *am* the canvas. I acquired the artwork for reasons of innocent distinction almost in direct contrast to the stereotypical whore or murderer only to become a one-time prostitute and failed assassin myself, which through the kaleidoscope effect boils down to the offensive body art. It obviously reveals the seeds of my discontent prior to the event or the failed event or the mere contemplation of an event. Two or three images form one.

The way they pontificate about assassins being losers in every conceivable fashion, they'd bring up my no-account jobs and the fact that I'm a bum without a goddamned prayer who, I now realize, only escaped these judgments through the irony of having been beaten to the draw in this folly of fucking misfits by Hinckley. That's society's revenge on the assassin or failed assassin: to undermine and ridicule his existence.

You can't just step outside experience, for everything you do is interpreted and categorized. One can't take an exit without inadvertently making a statement. If you refuse to participate you are shy or antisocial. If you resist the desire to shit you are displaying a retentive personality. If you bow out by killing yourself, then you're committing the act of suicide, which is fraught with connotations. If you're an assassin your tattoos are indicative of the sense of inferiority which supposedly motivates such pariahs, if you're a sailor they reflect your masculinity, and if you're a writer or painter—women, planets and palm trees might illustrate your bohemianism.

In the wake of Reagan's brush with death, I move to an inexpensive hotel in the French quarter. One night two spades in shades from Detroit are selling crystal meth in a bar. A couple of days later they approach me on the street very drunk, and having forgotten my face, now claim to be from New York, and that white shit has become coke. One man with no front teeth takes off his sunglasses and asks, "Want to fuck?"

I float north through St. Louis to Chicago, and check into a hotel on Madison West beside a Salvation Army. My room has pale green walls of flaking paint with running brown stains. Broken telephone, cupboard, empty mirror frame, dirty sink, radiator, old Bible, bare light bulb, ripped sheets serving as curtains. From the washroom down the hall one can see empty liquor bottles on the next roof.

I gaze out my window as darkness falls over the silhouettes of buildings and a water tower. The urban zone becomes black except for the twinkling lights of a little bar, and it's as if the world disappears beyond the bridge on the west side.

Then I start thumbing through the Bible. "Give glory to the Lord your God, before He cause darkness, and before your feet stumble upon the dark mountains, and, while ye look for light, He turn it into the shadow of death, *and* make *it* gross darkness."—Jeremiah 13, vs. 16. Looking out the window, I can see ultimate night.

"And be not drunk with wine, wherein is excess; but be filled with the Spirit;"—Ephesians 5, vs. 18. I raise the bottle to my mouth and look west at those glittering lights. Electric stars in the windy city.

The next day while returning from the art institute, I take the bus past my fleabag hotel and continue west along Madison, then across the bridge. It gets increasingly grimy, a skid row proper for what seems like miles of barren wasteland cluttered with bottles and zombies. Poor white trash get off at various stops as more Negroes board, and gradually my race thins out on the streets too. At this point I notice that the bus driver is also black.

Then I am the only Caucasian anywhere except for one blonde woman near the front who I am watching for blocks, wondering where she is going and finding solace in her presence until she stands up to get off too, and I see that it's a black woman in a blonde *wig*. I am the only whitey in a few square miles probably, although nobody seems to notice or care about the loner with the concealed gun looking out the window, not even the guy selling jewellery to the other passengers.

When we return along the same route, the races slowly inter-
mingle beneath an overcast sky while the engine rumbles and its
exhaust pollutes the air, and the streets are dirty and we are deep
in skid row again. I realize that I am indeed on the other side of
the bridge which spans River Styx, for this is the nether world
visible from my hotel room each night after the yellow sun
departs the heavens.

Later, while surveying the west side, I know that I've pene-
trated that darkness. I am safe in my lodgings with a Saturday
night special to bar evil from my door, cozy with the torn curtains and the two-cent light bulb. Stains on the cracked walls seem
liquescent. I hear sirens and peer outside to see eleven police cars
in a row screaming across the bridge down Madison West with
their cherries flashing.

I'll have to get rid of the .22. It seems to me that John
Hinckley has a real case for a refund on those devastator bullets.

In the meantime, I aim my gun at the tower and at the people loitering below. I have the power to relieve old men of their
misery. Maybe I'll just take out people who are rude to me. I can
put the barrel in my mouth and blow all my thoughts against the
filthy wall, but I look at those sparkling lights and I don't.

A Note On the Author

Among other things, Trevor Clark has worked as an oilrig rough-neck, editor, portrait photographer, bookstore manager, and home entertainment coordinator for a TV movie production company in the UK, where he lived for a number of years. He is an author of fiction, including *Born To Lose* (ECW Press), and his photographs have appeared in numerous publications. He currently lives in Vancouver.